A Church like Cluedo

Ray Filby

===
=

A Church like Cluedo

Publisher : Midhurst

Published by Midhurst

This is a work of fiction.

Any resemblance to actual persons, living or dead, is purely coincidental.

Midhurst.
2, Freers Mews,
Warwick,
Warwickshire,
CV34 6DP

Acknowledgements

The author would like to thank his wife Sue for her encouragement, patience and suggestions during the writing of this story.

Contents

Chapter 1

Annette Owen

"The post's arrived!"

Mrs. Owen, a lady in her early fifties called upstairs and then went back into the kitchen where she was sitting opposite her husband, a man of about the same age. They were about to eat a light breakfast consisting of cereal, toast and coffee. A third place had been laid. Mr. and Mrs Owen were on the point of starting breakfast when they had heard the sound of letters coming through the letter box and landing on the mat. Within seconds, a young woman, still in blue check pyjamas, rushed into the kitchen and picked up the pile of three letters which her mother had placed on her plate. The young woman was Annette, the seventeen year old daughter of the family. She hadn't had time to put on makeup but her lovely face hardly needed enhancement. She tossed back her shoulder length dark her as she looked at the first two letters, putting them aside, and hurriedly opened the third letter. This was the one her mother knew that Annette had been waiting for from the sender's name on the back of the envelope. As she unfolded the A4 sheet, Annette's anxious face suddenly changed to one of ecstatic delight.

"I've done it!" she declared as she handed the letter to her mother whose face had been as anxious as Annette's and she passed it on to Mr. Owen. On reading the contents, all their faces suddenly relaxed and became wreathed in smiles.

The letter informed Annette that she had been awarded an open scholarship to the Imperial College of Science and Technology, London University. Annette intended to take up a place at the City and Guilds of London Institute, one of the constituent colleges of the vast university which Imperial College had become, to study civil engineering. This was still an unusual choice of career for a woman although the gender demarcation in preferred courses for men and women was now becoming distinctly blurred.

The prayers of the Owen family had been wonderfully answered. Annette's hard work and study had been rewarded. The Owen family were devout Christians and were regular attenders at their local church of St. Giles. This had grown significantly in recent years as a result of the inspired ministry of the previous vicar, the Reverend Martin Jones. One of his regular themes was to insist that church-going alone did not make one a true Christian and he spent a lot of time in personal, one-to-one ministry, explaining the need for conversion and establishing a real and meaningful relationship with Jesus. Martin Jones endeared himself to the congregation by his hard work and preparedness to get his hands dirty if a difficult church job had to be done, whether it was clearing the church yard, painting the church hall or just being involved in preparing after-church refreshments. Mr. and Mrs. Owen were conscientious church workers and Annette was a Sunday school teacher. Martin Jones' example was very influential in leading Annette to adopt altruistic views on life.

When Mr. Jones retired, everyone realised that he would be a hard act to follow and his successor suffered from unfavourable comparison. The Revd. Thomas Fairbrother was not very active in his pastoral ministry and was reluctant to be involved in anything which involved the mundane manual tasks which were part of many church activities. He seemed to have the attitude that if he turned up on occasions in his best suit to see a working party getting on with a job, his presence as vicar would be encouragement enough. Mr. Fairbrother went round with a benevolent smile on his face but this mask soon slipped if ever he found himself crossed or opposed in any way. Annette's parents were concerned that Thomas Fairbrother's disappointing ministry might adversely affect Annette's enthusiasm. However, Annette was an objective thinker capable of independent thought. A few months after Mr. Fairbrother's appointment, Annette was off to university, her enthusiasm for service and positive living unabated.

During her three years at Imperial College, Annette performed well and was awarded the degree of B.Sc. (Eng.) with upper second class honours and the Associateship of the City and Guilds of London Institute (ACGI.). She had missed gaining a first by the narrowest of margins.

Annette had followed a course in civil engineering because she considered that she would gain a skill which she could use in serving a developing country overseas. During her college days, Annette had attended Holy Trinity, Brompton, a church near the college. Through the ministry of this church, Annette had experienced a profound development in her Christian faith.

Before seeking work in a developing country, she first needed industrial experience. Annette secured a job with Aztec Construction Ltd, a firm which had a long term contract for renovating roads in London. This meant that for the foreseeable future, Annette could stay in London without needing to move every few months. This would have been the case had she been working for a firm with short term road building contracts all over the country.

Annette rented a flat in a prosperous north London suburb and joined St. Augustine's, the local church. This church appeared to be a flourishing, operating from an impressive church building and boasting a large congregation. Annette soon discovered that in spite of its apparent prosperity, in many ways this church was severely lacking.

The Vicar, the Reverend Christopher Campbell, seemed an amiable enough character. He was now, very elderly and only a very few in the congregation could remember a time when Christopher Campbell had not been vicar of the church. Being elderly, he tended to be very traditional in his approach. He just didn't like change. Church services were based on the Book of Common Prayer, lessons were invariably read from the Authorised Version of the Bible and the pattern for Sunday services followed early morning Holy Communion, Morning Prayer at 11:00 a.m. and 6:30 p.m. Evening Prayer. When he walked round town, he always wore his black cassock. Mr. Campbell's leadership of the church seemed to be limited to officiating and preaching at Sunday services and chairing the meetings of the Parochial Church Council (PCC). However, he seemed to be greatly loved, even revered by the congregation. Had an alien come to this church to research religion on planet earth, he would have come to the conclusion that Christians worship a man who comes into church on Sundays dressed in special clothes and called the Vicar. Christopher Campbell preached sermons which were interesting, even intellectual, but without any real challenge. At one of the big events of the church's year, the Harvest Supper, the guests would arrive early to take their seats and await the arrival of Mr. Campbell who would be conducted to his seat at the top table by the churchwardens as the guests rhythmically clapped and the meal would start when the Vicar had pronounced a short grace.

The members of St. Augustine's were lovely, law abiding citizens but the unkind description of a Christian as somebody who believes in God, attends church on Sundays and is kind to their cat would not be far off the mark if they applied this definition to the members of St. Augustine's. Yes, they were regular church attenders. They involved themselves in the social life of the church but very few regularly read their Bibles or spent time in private prayer in their homes.

Most of the active work of the church was carried out by the curate, the Reverend Joe

Browning. He ran the youth club, carried out pastoral visiting, ran the confirmation class and led the cub pack as their Akela. This was one of the flourishing uniformed groups attached to the church. Although Joe's preaching may not have been as polished or as intellectual as the Vicar's, it was more challenging. Sadly, it was difficult to see any evidence of a positive response to these challenges.

Annette discovered that there was rather more ceremony at St. Augustine's than she had experienced at her previous churches of St. Giles and Holy Trinity, Brompton. One particular piece of ceremony which Annette found slightly amusing was the way the preacher was conducted to the pulpit by the verger who met the preacher at his stall, bowed, and led the Vicar to the pulpit pointing his wand in a forward direction. On reaching the pulpit steps, the verger would turn, bow to the preacher and wait while he climbed the eight or nine steps which led to the preaching platform. While Christopher obviously revelled in this piece of ceremony, Annette had the distinct feeling that Joe was not comfortable with this on the occasions when it was his turn to preach.

Annette soon became a popular member of St. Augustine's. She helped Joe with the running of the youth club and was always available to carry out work associated with the social activities run in the parish. After she had attended the church for a year, Annette was elected on to the PCC. An obvious gap in church provision which Annette had noticed was the absence of a Bible class for children of secondary school age to follow on from the church's Sunday School. She mentioned this to the Vicar and Curate. Christopher Campbell seemed strangely lukewarm but Joe Browning was keen on the idea and told Annette that this was something he had considered starting himself but as the only feasible time for running it was Sunday morning in parallel with the service of Morning Prayer, the Vicar had vetoed this as he considered that Joe's place was playing his part in running the morning service.

Annette raised the need to start a Bible class for children in the eleven plus age group at a PCC meeting but surprisingly, this suggestion was opposed by the Vicar. Annette felt that his objections didn't really hold water. His view was that once young people had started secondary school, they would be too busy with homework and church activities to attend a Sunday morning class and that it would probably undermine the work of the youth club. Further, there was no-one in the church with the right sort of experience to run such a group. Annette pointed out that far from undermining the work of the youth club which served the needs of young people who were sixteen plus, the Bible class would act as a feed of well instructed Christian young people to the youth club. Annette volunteered to run the Bible class and she pointed out that she had had experience in her previous church of assisting with the running of a Bible class. The Vicar continued to object but the PCC could see that his objections weren't valid. A vote was taken and it was almost unanimously decided that Annette should take responsibility for a Bible class for young people of secondary age. The class would start in church and remain with the Morning Prayer congregation until half way through the first hymn when the young people would move out into the church hall for learning activities suitable for children of secondary age. Annette made the sessions fun by devising exciting activities in which the children could become actively involved.

This was the first time that anyone could remember that a vote taken by the PCC had gone against the Vicar's wishes and he was clearly not pleased about this. Annette was able to recruit two devout middle-aged people, whom Annette would have described as 'tuned-in', to help her with the running of this class. It started well and quickly picked up momentum as its numbers grew to become a fairly major church activity.

Annette found herself on the opposite side to the Vicar when she suggested that a coach should be hired to take church members and others to hear Ambrose Augustus, an American evangelist in the Billy Graham mould, who was holding great rallies at a large stadium in London. The Vicar was scathing in his reaction to Annette's suggestion.

"Don't these American Evangelists know that the Christian church has been in England for over one thousand five hundred years? The

United States of America has only been in existence for two hundred years. Can't these American evangelists see that they just aren't needed in a country which is already Christian?"

Although they didn't have the full support of the Vicar, Annette and Joe organised a party of church members containing a high percentage from the youth club to hear Ambrose Augustus. Those attending this rally were visibly moved by the atmosphere in the stadium and the power of Ambrose Augustus' address. He presented them with the gospel and its implications as they'd never heard it before. Many made a commitment to Jesus Christ at the rally and everyone returned from the event a changed person. Joe apologised to Annette that he had not supported her more strongly against the Vicar at the PCC meeting but pointed out that he was reliant on a good recommendation from the Vicar if he was to move on and take over his own parish. He was delighted with the response so many of his youth club had made at the rally and felt that this provided him with a nucleus of vibrant Christian young people which would act like the leaven of the parable in permeating the youth club with young people, eager to witness to the Gospel's teaching.

A third issue between Annette and Christopher arose when she suggested the parish should run its own mission. The Vicar resolutely opposed this on the grounds that Sunday services were sufficiently well attended so that an influx of newcomers would over-stretch the available accommodation. A parish mission couldn't be launched without the Vicar's blessing.

As Annette considered the state of St. Augustine's, she felt that here was a church which was just drifting without achieving anything. At a PCC meeting she made her point by suggesting that the church should define some objectives to work towards. She emphasised her point by adding,

"Some churches have no objectives and they hit their target every time!"

This contribution did not please the Vicar.

"Of course we have objectives," he said. "Our main objective is to worship God!"

"This may be a laudable aim," countered Annette, "but it's an aim, not an objective. Three things are necessary in defining an objective. It must be measurable, it must be achievable and it must be time limited. For example, having an objective to treble the number attending church on a regular basis within a month would not be a sensible objective because although commendable and satisfying the first and third criteria, being realistic, it would be so unlikely to be achieved within the suggested time-scale that it would fail the second criterion."

The discussion struggled on a bit with no-one wanting to say anything they thought the Vicar might not approve of. Someone asked if getting fifty people to the next church social might count as an objective.

The Vicar immediately latched on to this.

"Thank you at last for raising something sensible to talk about."

The discussion moved on to talking about organising this social and any thought that the church might set some definable objectives to work towards was lost as the discussion centred on the logistics of this social which could be described as a monster bun fight. No record of the discussion on setting objectives occurred in the minutes of the meeting.

The church warden, who was known to toady to the Vicar, stated that in view of his training and over forty years' experience, the Vicar knows far more about running the church than any of us. Annette suspected the remark was aimed at her and thought to herself that if vicars are really such omnicompetent people, not needing the thoughts and ideas of others with a range of experience to help frame church policy, there would be no need for P.C.Cs. Christopher Campbell clearly wasn't up-to-date on current management principles. She rather mischievously thought further to herself that perhaps this Vicar hadn't had forty years' experience but one year's experience, forty times over.

Chapter 2

The Outcomes of Selection Committees.

Having gained a couple of years' post-graduate civil engineering experience, Annette felt that she was ready to offer herself for overseas service. She told the Vicar and Curate of her intention and asked if they would act as referees if she approached a missionary society. The conversation the Vicar, Christopher, had with his Curate, Joe, about Annette's request and about other developments in the church was typical of the Vicar's reactionary nature. The law had recently changed which allowed for the ordination of women which was very contrary to the Christopher's mind-set.

"The ordination of women is a disaster happening to the church before our eyes. St. Paul would turn in his grave if he saw women holding leadership positions in churches and preaching from the pulpit. Women don't seem to know their place anymore. Look at Annette, trained as an engineer! She's undoubtedly a talented young woman but what a waste of talent. Workers on a construction site won't be prepared to take instructions from a woman, however well qualified she may be. Perhaps things are different in the foreign parts where Annette seems intent on working."

Joe gently pointed out to the Vicar that inevitable changes in society were taking place. Women were already successfully doing jobs which had previously been considered exclusively male careers. There were now large numbers of women doctors and there had even been a woman prime-minister. He ventured to add that it may not be long before there are women bishops!

"Oh no!" retorted the Vicar. "That would be a step too far. I can't understand why these ordained women want to go by a male title. What's wrong with priestess? Deaconesses have been around for a long time so why do women want to switch to deacon. I call this clerical transgenderism! Even actresses seem to want to be referred to as actors! The world is changing for the worse!"

The Vicar huffed off into his cloud of yesteryear.

Annette applied to the Church Missionary Society (CMS) to investigate whether she could work with them as an associate missionary in a way which would enable her to use her professional skills in a developing country. Annette attended a CMS selection conference which was impressed with her dedication and educational background. They did not have missionaries serving abroad as civil engineers but considered Annette's qualifications and work in leading a Bible class at her church would fit her to do missionary work and teach physics at a fairly advanced level. They knew of a vacancy which had previously been filled by an associate missionary at a secondary school in Kerala State in India. Annette was advised to get the inoculations she would need to work in India but was warned that the Indian government was slow and even arbitrary in the matter of granting work visas. She had to be prepared for the fact that a visa may not be forthcoming. In the event that is what happened. After several months, the CMS contacted Annette to let her know that her visa application had been refused.

Annette took the disappointment well. She had been taught that if God closes a door, it's because there is a different door He wants to open for you. Annette felt that she should look out for what this alternative door might be.

While she enjoyed her work as a civil engineer and had no qualms about stepping out on pouring wet days to test the quality of recently laid tarmac or scrutinize road surfaces for slightly raised iron work, Annette was discovering that civil engineering was very much a man's world. She was respected by the men who worked under her but her only female company was the secretary who worked from the site porta-cabin. Annette was very much a 'people' person. It had not proved as easy as she had expected to secure a post working with people in a developing country by following her career overseas under the auspices of a Christian organisation. What might God really be calling her to do?

Her mind turned to the ordained ministry. Large numbers of women had now broken this previously male only taboo and were becoming ordained. As she thought of what she regarded as the shortcomings of the ministry at St. Augustine's and the differences she could make if she were in charge of a similar church, she became increasingly convinced that this is where God wanted her to be. The more she thought about it, the more this became an overriding ambition which could rightly be called a vocation.

She raised the matter with her Vicar but he was not enthusiastic about women entering the ministry and suggested that she should test her vocation by first training as a Reader in the Church of England. Annette worked out that that would delay her application for ordination by at least four years. She spoke to Joe who suggested that it might be a good idea if she consulted Canon Mark Hastings, the Diocesan Director of Ordinands, directly for his advice. Canon Mark was impressed with Annette and her record of church service. He asked her to complete a form of application, quoting three referees, one of which was to be her incumbent and no more than two of which were to be already in the ordained ministry.

In due course, Christopher Campbell provided a reference. It was very negative. Canon Hastings immediately phoned him back.

"Hello, Mr. Campbell. Canon Hastings here. Thank you for providing a reference for Annette Owen. It doesn't look very encouraging. Shall I contact her to let her know that her vicar doesn't think that she's a suitable candidate for the ministry?"

"Certainly not," came the blustering reply. "What I've written to you is confidential. Annette has a lot of loudly spoken friends in the parish and they would make life very difficult for me if it became known that I had obstructed her application for the ministry. Between you and me, I just think Annette's seeking the status which comes with ordination."

"Well, with the sort of reference you've given her, the selectors are certainly going to turn Annette down. They'll wonder why I've ever put her name forward."

"At the end of the day, it's their job to reject unsuitable candidates!"

"Yes, but they aren't there to do the vicar's dirty work for him. If you don't think she's suitable for the ministry, you should tell her to her face. You say that Annette is a disruptive influence on the PCC. Can you enlarge on that?"

"Oh, she pushes for things which may be all very well in their way but she fails to appreciate that the parish hasn't the manpower with the necessary skills to take on these enterprises and we can't afford to pay experienced staff from outside."

"What sort of enterprises are we talking about?"

"Oh, Bible classes, that sort of thing."

"Isn't there anyone in the parish who could take that on?"

"The only person who's volunteered is Annette herself and with her ideas, I don't really like her influencing our young people."

"What ideas?"

"Oh, it's no good thinking that living a good life is the way to heaven, that sort of thing."

Canon Hastings had heard enough.

"I can't help noticing Mr. Campbell that over the last forty years, there hasn't been a candidate for the ministry from St. Augustine's."

"No Indeed, that's very sad. There's just been no-one of the right calibre."

"Good day then, Mr. Campbell. Before I let Annette go to the selection conference, I will need to visit your PCC to ascertain what they think of Annette."

"Do you think that's necessary? OK, then, we can make that arrangement later."

The phone conversation ended. Canon Hastings was perplexed. On the face of it, Annette had seemed a very suitable candidate. She had remarkable references from other highly respected people she had cited but her Vicar seemed to have other opinions about her.

Canon Hastings arranged for other senior clerics to interview Annette before putting her name forward for selection and their impression was always positive. One of the questions she had been asked was whether the status of being ordained was important to her. Annette had replied,

"Yes, very important. The status of a minister of the gospel is that of a servant and as a minister, my prime aim would be to serve."

Canon Hastings attended a St. Augustine's PCC meeting where he could sound out grass roots opinion on Annette's suitability for the ministry. In spite of negative leading suggestions from the Vicar, the PCC were unanimously enthusiastic about Annette proceeding for ordination.

Canon Hastings had never had such a problem before in deciding whether or not to send a candidate for selection. In due course, Annette attended the selection conference. The day before attending the conference, Annette received a card from the Vicar wishing her good luck. This both pleased and rather surprised her as Annette had suspected that Christopher was perhaps lukewarm about her entering the ordained ministry

Annette soon made friends with the other candidates. She particularly noticed one of the candidates called Theophilus (Theo) Green. He seemed so enthusiastic. He always had something to say on any occasion he could make himself heard and had a loud penetrating voice which enabled him to dominate any group. He seemed particularly attracted to Annette and over the course of the selection conference, their friendship deepened. They arranged to meet up after the conference.

In the group discussions which the candidates held under the observant eyes of the selectors, they took it in turn to chair the group. Theo Green was always dominant in these discussions although much of what he said didn't always make a lot of sense. Annette was pleased with the way she had contributed to these discussions and particularly, in the way she had chaired the group, using the contributions made by her fellow candidates to bring the discussion to a clearly considered conclusion.

Annette was satisfied with the way she felt she had performed at the conference and came away, fully expecting that she would soon be informed of a positive outcome.

A few days after the conference ended, Annette was both surprised and disappointed to receive a letter informing her that she had not been recommended for ordination and an arrangement was made for her to meet Bishop Idris, the Suffragan Bishop of the diocese, to discuss the result.

The Bishop didn't come up with any valid reasons which could have justifiably explained Annette's rejection by the selection conference. He concluded the interview by saying that he felt Annette's personality was not up to her going ahead for the training which would lead to her ordination and he further stated that only first rate people were needed in the ministry. Annette didn't really fit the bill.

"You're so forthright and outspoken," he finally told her, "and you frequently disagree with figures of authority. You shouldn't ever apply to enter the ministry again! A person like you in the ministry would do great damage to the church!"

Annette had expected her Vicar to contact her to talk about the result of the selection conference but he didn't and Annette didn't contact the Vicar because she thought that it was his call to take the initiative in this matter. She told Joe about her experience and was surprised to find that Joe too had had been rejected by the selection committee when he had first made an application to be ordained.

"How is it then that you've come to be ordained?" she asked.

"The selection committee is only advisory and the bishop involved in my selection was a very different person from Bishop Idris. He said that he could see that I had great potential as a minister and ignored the negative recommendation of the selection committee."

Annette continued to talk about her rejection.

"I am surprised that the Bishop should end the interview with such hurtful, insensitive and offensive remarks to someone who was seeking to serve the church in the best way she could,"

"I don't think that the Bishop's attitude towards you came from the selection committee report," said Joe. "It is clear to me that you have been severely slandered but there's nothing you can do about it because it will all have been done under the cloak of confidentiality. Thus, no-one can be identified as the one who exerted a negative influence to prevent your ordination. The final decision has been made by the Bishop and a faceless committee who have been swayed more by a negative reference than your performance at the selection conference."

Joe continued with some very affirming words to Annette.

"Don't be too depressed by the Bishop's remarks. You are forthright and outspoken and this is not a negative but most commendable aspect of your personality as you're always courteous when you express your views. You are certainly polite in the way you express any disagreements and you do so with such logical clarity that people are easily persuaded to come round to your point of view."

There was one significant outcome of the selection conference for Annette. She started a serious relationship with Theo Green. Near the end of his first year at the theological college of St. Matthew and St. Mark, he asked Annette to marry him. Various things had cropped up during time she spent with Theo over the year which may have given Annette misgivings about marrying him. In many areas, he wasn't terribly communicative but she admired his apparent enthusiasm for ministry. Also she was attracted to the idea of being a clergy wife as the next best thing to ordination. Although Annette would doubtless have been a wonderful minister, some people have attributes which can be more usefully directed in God's service as a lay person than as a missionary or an ordained minister. There is no doubt that Annette had qualities which would make her the ideal clergy wife who would be a great asset to any parish where her husband served. Theo and Annette were married during the summer break at the end of Theo's first year of theological study. It is likely that the prospect of becoming a minister's wife weighed more heavily with Annette in her decision to marry Theo than a deep love for Theo. Theo had dark secrets which Annette was not to discover until many years later.

There were married quarters associated with the college and Annette fitted in more than well as the wife of a student at the college. She formed good relationships with the college staff and the wives of the other students. Annette seemed to possess a serene wisdom which the other wives noticed and they often came to Annette for counselling when difficulties and frustrations arose in their lives. Annette's wise counsel usually went a long way to solving the problem.

Chapter 3

Cleared for Ordination

"We can't let Theophilus Green go ahead for ordination, surely not! He's just not up to it."

This damning comment was made by the Reverend Dr. Edwin Harmsworth, senior lecturer at St. Matthew's and St. Mark's Theological College, a college which admitted both men and women ordinands. Dr. Harmsworth was a tall lean ascetic cleric who was probably in his early fifties. He somehow managed to combine the conflicting attributes of having sharp features but a kindly face. He wore a smart well pressed grey suit over his black clerical shirt and collar. Edwin was sitting at a table next to the Reverend Dr. William Tudor Jones, principal of the college. Dr. Jones' appearance contrasted with his younger colleague. He was rotund, - some unkindly said, overweight. He was nicknamed 'Tubby Jones' by the students. Dr. Jones was a jolly, easy going sort of fellow with no fashion sense. He wore a predominantly brown check jacket over his pale blue clerical shirt and collar which did not go well with his ill-fitting navy blue trousers.

Both Edwin and William had moved into lecturing posts in this theological college after completing successful ministries in difficult inner city parishes in the north of England. They had earned considerable academic reputations, Edwin at Cambridge for his work on the contrasting poetical styles of the minor Old Testament prophets and William at Oxford on the New Testament apocryphal books. They were now in William's spacious office, not sitting opposite one another across William's desk but side by side at a large table covered with papers. These represented the accumulated work of the twenty or so students who had completed their studies and were preparing to enter the ministry.

Although fairly large, the office had a cluttered appearance. The book shelves were well stocked with theological tomes but a large number of books had found their way out of the bookshelves, on to chairs, on to William's desk where they were accumulated in untidy piles, and several were strewn about on the floor, waiting to be returned to their correct location in the book shelves. Principal Tudor Jones was not a tidy worker but very efficient and effective. The Holy Spirit has been described in similar terms.

The Principal came to the defence of Theophilus (Theo) Green.

"Theo may not be academic but he's frightfully keen. He may be a duffer at New Testament Greek but we've had other students who couldn't cope with the language who have gone on to become excellent ministers."

"I agree," replied Edwin. "Not knowing Greek is not a serious handicap to a minister in this day and age but Theo has performed badly at everything. This cohort of students is the weakest we've had for a long time but Theo comes way down at the bottom. He covers this with a façade of enthusiasm but I think that's just a pose to impress us. He seeks to demonstrate his enthusiasm by volunteering for anything which comes up, even activities to which he is not particular suited, and then he uses the fact that he is involved in these voluntary activities as an excuse for handing in his essays late! If he was really keen, he'd spend a bit more time in his study and less socialising, and we might have had better results over the year."

"Well, ability to mix well with others is a prime quality in a minister. Theo perhaps realises this and has used his time at college to develop the inter-personal skills which will be so valuable when he's in a parish."

"For all the time Theo spends at the snooker table, on the croquet pitch, and playing cards, he somehow doesn't seem to be a popular student. I can't put my finger on it but I've noticed that Theo is always the one having to join a group. Students don't spontaneously go and spend the time of day with Theo."

William replied with a twinkle in his eye.

"Here we are, discussing Theo like hard cop, soft cop in an American police drama. After the money that's been spent on preparing Theo for the ministry, you know that we would have to answer some very serious questions about what we've been doing over the past three years if we oppose Theo going forward for ordination at this stage. He has another phase of training to go through as a deacon in the parish to which he's assigned."

"When he's in a parish! I find so many of our students who consider they have a calling to the ministry, have no clear idea as to what is the responsibility to which they'll become inducted when they take over a parish. So many of them are limited to believe their job is no more than to run a church, conduct services according to canon law and provide pastoral care for those who attend church. Very few recognise that the responsibility which they share with the bishop, is the care of souls within their parish, and that includes everyone, not just the church goers. When our students are inducted as deacons, they'll assume the title of curate of whatsoever church they are attached to. Language has changed its meaning over the years. When I first entered the ministry, although referred to as curate, my official title was Assistant Curate. The actual curate, the one with ultimate responsibility for the care of souls of all living within the boundaries of his parish, was known as the Vicar or Rector.”

“You’re right. That’s a dread responsibility we all undertake in entering parish ministry. How does one fulfil that responsibility? I don’t like the practice of cold calling so, in the parishes where I have served, I have used the local electoral register to write a personally addressed letter to every household living in the parish who didn’t already have a connection with church. I offered to meet them personally to talk about any matter they might like to raise.”

“Was this successful?” asked Edwin.

“Only to a very limited extent but I made really useful contacts with the few who did make a positive reply to my invitation. How many of our students will interpret their responsibility as curators of souls in their parish in the same way as ourselves?” asked William.

Edwin paused thoughtfully before replying.

"Very few, if any, will see their responsibility extending far beyond those who actually attend church. Your vision was not limited to serve only the regular churchgoers as you attempted to make personal contact with everyone living within the parish boundary. No one could criticise you for not doing the utmost to seek out the lost sheep when you were in parish ministry but as you said, only a few responded. Jesus warned the disciples he sent on missions that they would face rejection at some of places they called. No, I'm sad to say that I think only a few of our students will adopt the same attitudes that we held when running a parish. I would support most strongly any student who demonstrated a really strong yearning to win souls in his quest to enter the ministry, regardless of his academic performance at college."

"Does Theo fall into this category?"

"From the conversations I have had with him, I feel he pays no more than lip service to these ideals. Perhaps I may have a blind prejudice against him because I never really took to him from the day he joined St. Matthew's and St.

Mark's. However, there is another aspect of his character which disturbs me and makes me feel uneasy about letting him loose as a Christian minister. He's just downright dishonest, and he's so stupid in the lies he tells. When I challenged him about an essay he'd submitted as part of his ethics module which was almost copied verbatim from the internet, he said it was not surprising that serious thinking minds who have contemplated this subject should arrive at the same conclusions."

William laughed, coughed and immediately reassumed his serious face.

"No, indeed, this is not really a laughing matter. I share your concerns regarding Theo's integrity as a person. When I challenged him as to why he'd missed a tutorial with me, he said he had been to Lichfield to research some information on the Saxon saints of Mercia and had missed the bus back. I knew that that was untrue because I'd seen him on the croquet pitch on my way to my study to conduct the tutorial. I should have challenged him but I didn't want to embarrass the fellow any more than he clearly already was through missing the tutorial. I don't know what he'd learnt at Lichfield, if indeed he ever went there, but he managed to confuse St. Chad and St. Cedd in the essay he submitted on the subject."

"Well then, do we let him proceed?"

This time, the Principal thought long and carefully before replying.

"There is another factor in Theo's favour which we haven't considered. He has a most exceptional wife. She has supported the wives of other students when they have been going through a difficult patch. She's kindly, considerate, charming and energetic. She would make the most wonderful clergy wife."

"You're absolutely right about Annette. In days gone by, many girls saw marrying a priest as their call to ordination. Fortunately, women are no longer barred from ordination and have no need to follow this backdoor route into ministry. I wish Annette had sought ordination herself. There are many clergy ladies now who are themselves married to ministers. Yes, Theo is very fortunate in being married to someone who'll be such an asset to him in his ministry."

(Dr, Harmsworth was unaware that before she met Theo, Annette herself had been a candidate for the ministry, or that she had actually met Theo at a selection conference.)

"Theo has already been passed as fit for the ministry by the Bishop and the selection conference he attended. Indeed, the selection committee regarded him as an excellent candidate. Our job is primarily to develop the skills and impart the theological knowledge to our students which they will need in their ministries. We have let students through whose academic performance has been nearly as poor as Theo's and they have made a success of their ministries. Yes, I believe we must allow him to proceed with our blessing. However, we'll need to consult very carefully with the Bishop and Archdeacon in deciding which incumbent is best fitted to give Theo further guidance as he serves his title as a curate before going on to take full responsibility for a parish."

Edwin suggested a compromise.

"OK! We allow him to go ahead for ordination but we don't award him a college associateship. Someone like Theo describing himself as Associate of St. Matthew's and St. Mark's would downgrade the academic status of our college. The only real difference this will make to Theo is that he won't be able to wear the college hood over his cassock and surplice. However, that's not going to make much difference to Theo. Being of a high church leaning, I imagine he'll conduct most services wearing a cassock alb and cope."

So it was that Theo Green was ordered as a deacon and allocated a curacy in a parish which in Anglican terms would be described as 'middle of the road' in its ministry.

Chapter 4

St. James, Irminghampton

Thus, the Reverend Theophilus Green became assistant curate at the parish of St. James in the small country town of Irminghampton. His vicar was the Reverend Henry Sylvester, a very experienced parish priest who had guided several deacons through their curacies and on to become fully ordained ministers. How would Theo fare under Mr. Sylvester?

Theo fared surprisingly well in view of the misgivings which had been expressed by the senior staff at his theological college. He displayed considerable enthusiasm for anything his vicar suggested. He showed some initiative in starting up social events, weekly ballroom dance evenings, quiz sessions, country rambles and treasure hunts around the parish. However, the Parochial Church Council (PCC) would not give him the go-ahead to launch afternoon bingo sessions for the elderly.

One of the main difficulties experienced by Theo and his Vicar lay in homiletics. Theo could stand up and preach at length but his sermons were just a cascade of words delivered with perfect syntax but devoid of deep meaning. Henry Sylvester had experienced this problem before with his curates. Theological colleges were not always successful in this aspect of their training. Henry Sylvester realised that Theo would need more guidance than most in the matter of delivering meaningful sermons and at the end of the year, Theo showed some improvement, but he was obviously never going to be a really good preacher. The imagination he showed in organising social events did not transfer to his sermon preparation.

As the senior staff at St. Matthew's and St. Mark's had predicted, Annette Green proved herself to be an ideal clergy wife. She hit it off from the word go with Mrs. Sylvester. There were gaps in the provision for women at St. James. Mrs. Sylvester ran the Mothers' Union but this largely consisted of women over the age of fifty. While many of the younger women had jobs, there were quite a few whose husbands were sufficiently well paid that they didn't need to work and they found plenty of voluntary work to keep them busy and to challenge their talents. Most of these young women would have welcomed a church based activity during the day time to meet up but knew they would feel out of place among the older women at the Mothers' Union. Seeing this gap, Annette Green started a Young Wives group which proved very popular with the younger women who had distanced themselves from the Mothers' Union. One evening a week, Annette ran a Bible study group in their two bedroom curate's house. This soon proved so popular that the group had to be split and run on two separate evenings. This was an aspect of ministry in which Theo showed no special interest so Annette ran both groups. As both groups were following the same Bible study course, Annette found her preparation was sufficient to cover the needs of both groups.

The uniformed organisations, Scouts, Guides, Cubs, Brownies, Beavers and Rainbows were already well staffed and met in the evenings at the fairly modern church centre. There was a flourishing Sunday School too, run by Mrs. Sylvester with a dedicated group of teachers. However, this stopped at the age of eleven.

There was a gap in the provision of Christian education for the eleven pluses. Annette teamed up with the wife of the Church Warden, Muriel Moncaster, to run a Bible Class on Sunday mornings for those in secondary school. This ran in parallel with the main Sunday morning service. After running for a year, this group became affiliated to the national organisation for similar groups called Pathfinders.

The three years of Theo' curacy passed very pleasantly and productively at St. James. Theo had only one serious falling out with his vicar and this arose from his tendency to say the first thing which came into his head when he was put on the spot, regardless of whether or not it was true. Theo was on the rota to lead the prayers on the Ascension Day service but as it didn't fall within his usual weekly schedule, Theo had overlooked the fact that he was needed at this evening service and forgot to turn up. When the Vicar had challenged Theo about his absence, it would have been far better for Theo to simply admit that he'd forgotten. However, Theo said that he'd heard that Mrs. Elizabeth Jenkinson, and elderly parishioner, was seriously ill and felt he had to visit her.

Things had turned out more difficult than he'd expected and by the time he was able to leave Mrs. Jenkinson, it was too late to get to the evening service. Theo was very red faced with nowhere to turn when Mr. Sylvester told him that Mrs. Jenkinson had actually made her way to the Ascension Day evening service!

At the end of his three years, Theo was inducted as Vicar of St. Thomas, Barnholme. This was a prosperous church in the diocese of Marlincester. The parishioners of Irminghampton had become quite fond of the Greens over the time they'd spent in the parish and they collected to give them a generous leaving present. A coach had been hired for the occasion and most of the members of St. James Church made their way to Barnholme to see their former curate inducted into his new living.

Chapter 5

St. Thomas's, Barnholme

Theo and Annette settled very quickly into their new living at Barnholme. There was already a lot going on there on the social side but Theo extended these by starting ballroom dancing evenings, woodwork classes for the men and cookery classes for the ladies. This time, he was allowed by the PCC to start Bingo afternoons for the elderly. Annette took over the Pathfinder Bible class into which children moved up from the Sunday School on reaching secondary age. She held Bible studies one evening a week in the Vicarage. The equivalent of a Young Wives' group was already running well and the Mothers' Union was well established.

St. Thomas's was a very prosperous church. Collections at main services were always of the order of several hundred pounds and on special occasions, exceeded a thousand pounds. The church had no difficulty in paying its parish share. This had a consequence which Theo found very annoying. The parish share was steadily increased, year by year to far above what was demanded of other parishes of a similar size and socio-economic grouping. He hit upon a very ingenious idea, ingenious but not ethical, to counter this.   Without the knowledge of the church wardens, he took the alms dish to a firm, highly reputed in the manufacture of bespoke metal goods. This required a long journey as the firm was located some way from Barnholme. He told Annette the half-truth that he needed to visit his elderly uncle whom he called in on when he had completed his business at the metal workers. The firm assured Theo that they could replicate such a dish. It would be expensive but when made, you wouldn't be able to tell the copy from the original. Theo had come with a high definition photograph of the alms dish so he didn't need to leave the original at the metal workers. He returned the original dish to the church safe when he returned during the evening of the same day.

Theo also had a very special trolley made up at a firm of specialist furniture manufacturers, again, located many miles from Barnholme. This trolley was to be made of oak. Its special feature was that immediately below the top, there were to be two shelves, one above the other. Each of these shelves was to be deep enough to hold an alms dish holding a complement of collection bags, completely filled with the money received as collection during a service. Three sides of the shelves were to be completely covered with oak panels. The fourth side was to be constructed to contain a sliding oak panel which could be slid, up or down to seal off either of the two shelves. When the panel was in either position, provision was to be made to lock the panel in place by a pair of bolts which were invisible from the outside but which could be manually operated from the inside of the front legs of the trolley. This again was not an inexpensive thing to manufacture but it was going to more than pay for itself.

When this trolley was received at St. Thomas's, Theo demonstrated it to the churchwardens and to those who acted as servers at services of Holy Communion. He explained that the idea was to make their work easier. The flagons, chalices, patens, wine bottles and flasks would be taken from the safe in the vestry before a service, loaded on to the trolley and wheeled into church from whence the communion vessels would be transferred to the communion table or altar as it is known in many churches. When he received the alms dish near the end of the service, the Vicar would bless the donations and transfer the plate to the shelf near the top of the trolley. At the end of the service, the communion vessels would be loaded back on to the trolley and wheeled back to the vestry where the vessels would be removed for washing and the alms dish taken to the table where two sides-persons would count the collection under the supervision of the churchwardens.

The feature of the trolley which Theo did not disclose was the fact that there were two shelves, either but not both of which could be concealed behind a panel, secured in position by a cunningly concealed bolts behind the front trolley legs.

This innovation of the trolley was welcomed by the wardens and servers, unaware of the secret that had been built in. It could be seen immediately that it would greatly facilitate the movement of communion vessels to and from the vestry, before and after the service.

Now the device could be tried out for the purpose which Theo had intended. On the Saturday, Theo filled eight of the collection bags with money he had carefully saved up to about 90% of the money usually expected as collection during a communion service. (There was no shortage of collection bags at St. Thomas's. Of the twenty or so bags stored in the vestry, only eight bags were in use during the Sunday services. The sides-persons used these to take the collection from different parts of the congregation during the final hymn according to a pattern designed by the churchwardens.) Theo placed the bags he had filled on the duplicated alms dish whose existence was known only to himself and placed the dish on the upper of the two shelves on the communion trolley. He then slid the panel upwards and secured it in position with the concealed bolts.

On Sunday, the service of Holy Communion ran its usual course. On receiving the collection, Theo raised the alms dish before the congregation as he consecrated the gifts and then slid the dish on to the open lower shelf of the trolley. He deftly operated the bolts so that the panel slid down from the top to the bottom shelf and secured it in position. This action was carried out at the back of the trolley and hence, out of sight to everyone except Theo. At the end of the service, the trolley was wheeled out and the alms dish on the top shelf taken out for the collection to be counted with no-one suspecting that the actual alms dish used in the service was still concealed in the trolley.

This procedure was carried out every Sunday, The day after the service, Theo took ten percent of the collection concealed in the trolley and returned the remainder to the upper shelf of the trolley where it remained concealed until taken for counting the following Sunday. Theo had taken what he euphemistically called his tithe. This action was deplorable on two counts. It didn't just depress the apparent size of the collection to dissuade the diocesan officers from demanding a realistic parish share from St. Thomas's. The ten percent taken from the collection was retained by Theo himself. He didn't even pay the money into his bank account which would have created a trace, should the finances ever be scrutinised to that amount of detail. He used the money for his day to day expenses. Theo had developed the perfect way to launder the stolen money. The one tell-tale piece of evidence which would only have been noticed by someone looking for it and putting two and two together, was that the collection mysteriously increased by about ten percent on Sundays when Theo was not officiating at the Holy Communion service! However, as the Sunday collections fluctuated by about fifteen percent from week to week, this was hardly noticed. Indeed, the Sundays when Theo was not taking the services at St. Thomas's were invariably holiday periods when the congregation, and therefore the collection, was lower than usual anyway.

Chapter 6

WPC Joan Powers

Having graduated with a good honours degree in physics from Manchester University, Joan Powers had worked for a few years with a firm developing fibre optics interfaces between computers. She decided she wanted a more active life style and decided to enter the police force. After completing the training course at Hendon Police Academy with flying colours, she joined the constabulary. Joan Powers was now a lady police officer with three years' experience on the strength of Oakentown Police station. She was a committed Christian and attended the local Anglican Church of St. Andrew's.

Joan was competent, popular among the other police officers, very efficient and someone who really enjoyed her job. Her beat partner was PC Colin Whittaker, an equally dedicated cop. When they chatted as they strolled the beat in Oakentown, their discussion was on police matters rather than just small talk. They had both had drummed into them while at Hendon

Police Academy the importance of being observant when on duty, and not much missed them as they patrolled the streets.

"Mrs. Thompson hasn't taken her milk in yet. She's usually up and about by now. We'd better check on that later in the day," commented Colin as they walked by a terrace of Victorian houses.

"That car's dangerously parked on the corner," observed Joan. "There's plenty of safer places to park down the street. I think we'd better find the owner."

They called on the nearest house. The owner looked alarmed as he opened the door to see two police officers standing there.

"Yes?" He spoke the word as a query.

"Don't look alarmed. This is only a call to be of help. Is that your car parked on the corner?"

"No, it's my son's."

"We would suggest he parks it a bit further down the street, away from the corner. It's not illegally parked but traffic turning right won't have a clear view down the street as they make this manoeuvre with your son's car parked there. Also, a lot of heavy lorries turn here and the car stands in risk of getting damaged if it stays where it is now."

"Thank you," said the man who had answered the door, relieved that he hadn't unwittingly been involved in some crime that was being investigated.

They turned from the residential area into Oakentown High Street. They stopped by a couple of bikes which lay sprawled across the pavement. They called out to some youths talking and laughing loudly nearby.

"Are these your bikes?"

The youths suddenly fell silent.

"Well, they shouldn't be left lying on the pavement like that. They're a danger to passersby. Show a bit of consideration and park them by a wall or lamp-post."

Two of the youths left the group, sheepishly picked up the bikes and re-parked them, following the police officers' instructions.

As they continued down the high street, Joan pointed out to Colin that the blue Mercedes they were approaching was often seen parked there. Nothing terribly strange in this except that it was never empty but always occupied by a driver who seemed to be closely observing what was going on. She had made a note of the number but had also adopted an old police trick of memorising the number, GF 06 PAM, by mentally constructing a little verse whose words rhymed with the number and whose initial letters were the letters on the car's number plate. She had found this useful on occasions when she had been required to instantly recall a car number.

GO FIX,   ZERO SIX,   PICK AND MIX

Colin had made a similar observation about the white Astra, parked on the other side of the road. He had similarly made a mental note of the number, ND 11 HSF

NONE DONE, ONE ONE, HAVE SOME FUN

"The reason I have taken note of something which might seem very ordinary," continued Colin, "is that on occasions, I've seen the drivers of these cars sitting together in one or other of the two cars in earnest discussion. One of them clearly drew the attention of the other to the fact that we were passing by!"

"Well," replied Joan, "We make a point of varying our route so we don't pass the same point at the same time each day. If they are up to no good, they won't be able to anticipate a time when we won't be around."

"There's not much here to be a focus for big time crime," commented Colin.

"Lloyd's Bank is a long way further down the street," observed Joan, "but 'Fair-Bet' betting shop is only just along the road. That's always busy. They must have fairly big takings. When do they bank their money?"

"A security van calls most Tuesdays. They're not as careful as we are about varying the times they collect the cash."

"You're right about that Colin. I've noticed the security van outside the betting shop on those occasions when we happen to be here It arrives invariably between three and four o'clock in the afternoon.

A couple of weeks later, Joan and Colin were patrolling Oakentown High Street mid-afternoon. The security van was waiting outside the betting shop. The security guards came out of the shop carrying their reinforced cases containing the betting shop takings over the past week. Suddenly a group of men rushed out of the betting shop, running towards the van. One of the security guards scuttled across the road with his heavy security case to the waiting Astra, climbed in and the engine revved as the driver prepared to speed away. Joan realised that a crime was being committed. She dashed across the road and flung herself across the Astra's bonnet. The Astra gathered speed. Joan clung on to the car's wing mirror. The car started to weave backwards and forwards in an attempt to dislodge Joan. Joan was across the windscreen. The driver was driving blind. He struck a lamppost head on. Joan was thrown off the bonnet on to the pavement by the impact. The driver and passenger got out and ran off down a side street. Joan was bruised but not seriously injured. She got up and gave chase. Her quarry was well ahead. They separated and ran down different side streets. By the time Joan reached the point where they had separated, they were out of sight, having turned off into other side streets further down the roads at which they had exited.

Joan realised that chasing further was futile and she limped back to the high street. It was only now apparent to Joan that her leg had been badly bruised as the car impacted the lamp post. By the time she got back to the high street, it was a flurry of police activity. Colin had radioed headquarters for assistance and two police cars had soon arrived on the scene. The apparent security man who hadn't run away was in custody, the Astra was a crumpled wreck against a lamp post some way down the street and the blue Mercedes was nowhere to be seen.

Chapter 7

A disappointment for the Chief Constable

The following day, when Joan and Colin returned to the police station for duty, details of the crime became apparent. The security van was not a real security van but just an ordinary van, painted to look like one. A car had drawn up in front of the real security van when it was on its way and about half-a-mile from the betting shop, causing it to stop. Two men had got out of the car, shot the security van's tyres, and driven off before the genuine security men could get a good look at the car's number plates. They were probably false number plates anyway. Meanwhile, outside the betting shop, two bogus security men had got out of the van and called in to the betting shop to collect the money. The betting shop owner was a bit suspicious as these weren't the usual security officers who collected the takings, but security personnel did change from time to time. They were properly kitted up with helmets and protective clothing. They had left the shop with the money and would have got clean away had not the guards in the real security van phoned through to the shop just as the thieves were leaving. They warned the betting shop owner that in view of what had just happened to their van, something untoward was going on. Men from the shop joined the manager in rushing out and they managed to get to the men before they made their getaway. Joan and Colin of course were quickly on the scene. The criminal who had got to the Astra before Joan could apprehend him had left the case containing the stolen money in the Astra as he ran off with his associate when the car had crashed into the lamp post. The case was thus recovered, much to the relief and gratitude of the betting shop owner.

Now came the task of identifying the perpetuators of this crime. The bogus security man who hadn't run away from the scene wasn't much help. He was a petty criminal involved in small time crime but nothing big. He'd been approached in a pub by a man, purporting to be from the security firm, who was recruiting someone who would be prepared to step in as a temporary replacement for a security employee who had reported sick and was needed that day to collect money from the betting shop. He went to an office where he had a short interview and was supplied with the security helmet and protective clothing, and here he was in police custody, having had no idea that he had been recruited to take part in a robbery. It was discovered that the office where the interview had taken place had been rented for one day only and the person making the rental couldn't be traced.

The car number of the white Astra was of no help. This was a stolen car bearing false number plates. There was no fingerprint evidence. Joan then volunteered that she had taken the number of the blue Mercedes which she and Colin had good reason to believe was involved in the crime. This was a good lead. The Mercedes wasn't stolen and so the police had the address where the car was registered. A search warrant was issued and the police made a surprise visit to a large mansion in the fashionable part of a county town. They struck gold. In their search. They discovered evidence which linked the owner of the house to a number of unsolved crimes, together with the planning details of further crimes. Joan and Colin were able to identify the owner of this house as the man they had seen waiting near the betting shop in the blue Mercedes.

After a few days, the pain from her bruised leg subsided and the blue bruise gradually faded. The Superintendent invited Joan into his office.

"I want to congratulate you on the way you responded to the incident last Tuesday when you put yourself at considerable risk. You have demonstrated the very best in police work in your perceptive observation and the way you noted the number of a car whose owner you suspected might be up to not good. Without that number, it would have taken us very much longer to track down the brains behind quite a few criminal enterprises. The Chief Constable wants to issue you with a special commendation for your exemplary dedication to duty. You have been marked out for going far in the police service."

Joan then dropped what for the superintendent was a bombshell.

"I have decided to leave the police service, sir."

The Superintendent was aghast.

"I do hope the experience you had on Tuesday hasn't alienated you from being a police woman. You've a great future ahead in the police service you know."

"Not at all, sir. I really enjoyed being involved in the way I was last Tuesday. It was just the sort of thing I came into the police service for. However, I now have my eyes fixed on quite a different career."

"Tell me more."

"Some of my work with the police has brought me into contact with a side of life about which I had no previous first-hand knowledge. My beat has taken me through some of the poorer areas in Oakentown where I have got to know the people there. Many of them are very sad people, drifting in and out of debt, experiencing marital problems, having problem kids they can't control. They're drifting through life with no hope for the future in this life or beyond. I feel called to serve people like this as a minister of the church, to give them hope and encouragement, regardless of the difficult times they're facing. Sadly, so many affluent people have decided that they don't need faith but these poorer people desperately do and I think that in the role of a minister, I will be in a position to share my faith with them."

What could the Superintendent say after Joan had poured out this personal heartfelt need?

"Very well. You will go with my blessing and that of everyone here at Oakentown police station. The Chief Constable will be very disappointed but I know he will give you any support you need."

"One other thing," continued Joan, "my sister has just completed her course at Hendon Police Academy and from what I have told her, I know that she would like to come here to Oakentown. She looks just like me," said Joan with a smile, "so if you'll have her, perhaps that'll help you pretend that I'm still here."

Chapter 8

A Remarkable Ordinand.

Three years later, Edwin Harmsworth and William Tudor Jones were in the Principal's study, undertaking their annual task of reviewing the students about to pass out of St. Matthew's and St. Mark's Theological College. This batch of ordinands appeared to be an improvement on those which had been discussed three years earlier when Theo Green had narrowly escaped being failed at this last hurdle. Edwin and William looked much the same as they had done three years earlier with no serious sign of further ageing. Once people reach middle age, their appearance often seems to reach a plateau and the ageing process can then seem to be very gradual. The office looked just as untidy as it had three years earlier!

"This batch of students has been really exceptional," started Edwin. "There's not a lame duck among them. Indeed, there have been some quite outstanding individuals."

"I'm sure that you would include Joan Powers in that group of outstanding students," added the Principal. "I've been really impressed with that young woman's all-round ability. She shines academically, she relates well to everyone she meets and her sermons are exceptional. We're here to teach the likes of her, but as she preaches, I feel that I'm learning new things from her all the time."

"Me likewise," agreed Edwin. "The church no longer has a glass ceiling, limiting how far a woman may advance in its hierarchy so I fully expect that one day, Joan will become a bishop."

"I certainly hope that that may happen," responded the Principal. "Very few of our students have advanced that far in their careers but this time, I think we may have a candidate bound for the episcope. I'm so glad she came here rather than one of the Oxbridge colleges. They would have awarded her a fellowship and encouraged her to remain in academia."

"There'd be no chance of that," responded Edwin. "She has a clear sense where her vocation is going to take her and it's working among people, not among books"

"Do we know where she's going to serve her title?"

"St. Thomas's, Barnholme."

"Who's the vicar there? Is he one of our former students?"

"Yes, - wait for it," Edwin paused for effect. "Theo Green!"

William winced.

"Whatever does the Bishop think he's doing, sending a brilliant student like Joan to work under someone I used to think of as a duffer?"

"Apparently, the parish is running well under Theo. I rather think Annette will have made a big contribution to that, but I think there is another strand to the Bishop's thinking. He knows that Joan will pick up the mechanics of running a parish, relating to the PCC, conducting services and so on, whatever the parish to which she is assigned. However, sending a really able curate to a parish with a lame duck vicar can sometimes work marvels in improving the ministry of that vicar. I rather think that the Bishop wants to see if Joan can effect this transformation in Theo."

"Well, I'm sure the Bishop knows what he's doing," concluded the Principal.

Edwin and William then went on to review the work of other students about to be launched into parish ministry.

Chapter 9

DS Christine Powers

Soon after Joan's departure from Oakenhampton, her sister, Christine started her police career at the same station after performing as an exemplary student at Hendon Police Academy. She was so like her sister in many, many ways that it was just like having Joan back on the strength of Oakenhampton police station. Her ability and hard work saw Christine rise fairly rapidly in the ranks and after just a few years, she was a Detective Sergeant, serving under Detective Inspector Colin Whittaker who had been Joan's beat partner in her early days as a Woman Police Constable.

Christine showed the flair and imagination which enabled many cases on the Oakenhampton books to be cleared up very effectively and quickly. A particular case which illustrates Christine's flair arose when the Superintendent at Oakenhampton was approached by the local branch of Canterbury's supermarket chain to help clear up a case of shoplifting. It was unusual for the police to be approached to help in their security surveillance as Canterbury's had their own security staff who were pretty efficient at their jobs. The self-checkout tills had led to a certain amount of theft as it was easy for dishonest customers to slip extra items into their shopping bags which had not been recorded on the scanner. However, the saving in staff wages which had accompanied the introduction of self-checkout tills, more than compensated for the increased theft that had followed this innovation. But now, shoplifting had suddenly shown a dramatic and unsustainable increase which Canterbury's security staff had been unable to stem, even with increased vigilance.

A meeting was arranged between the local Canterbury's store manager, Mr. Lennox, and the plain clothes police officers at Oakenhampton headed by DI Colin Whittaker. DS Christine Powers of course was there. Mr. Lennox explained the security systems already in place. The closed circuit television (CCTV) surveillance of the shopping aisles and entrance was continuously monitored by a member of the security staff sitting near the entrance of the shop and watching a monitor. Detectors at the entrance to the shop and at the customer toilets would respond if a trolley was wheeled out containing an item from which the security tag had not been removed. A close watch was being kept on the self-checkouts but this was only able to minimise and not eliminate the relatively small amount of theft occurring at these checkouts. However, the scale of theft now being experienced was far in excess of the relatively small number of items which could be filched at the self-checkout locations. Mr. Lennox mentioned that on one occasion, a woman had been stopped from leaving the store with a very full trolley because the security staff didn't think she'd gone through any checkout but she showed them her receipt which matched the last four digits on her credit card and when her trolley was examined, all the items matched the receipt.

DI Whittaker asked Mr. Lennox if other branched of Canterbury's had experienced a similar problem.

Mr. Lennox explained, "There were seven major branches of Canterbury's in the locality.

Of these, only the ones at Cavinshaw and Nettleford were experiencing similar problems. An alarming increase in shoplifting had occurred in these branches at about the same time as at his shop in Oakenhampton."

DS Christine Powers immediately noticed a connection.

"The three stores experiencing this problem all have a well-known branch of a chain of coffee shops adjacent to Canterbury's which may be directly accessed from Canterbury's without the customer having to go out into the street first," she observed.

"That's right," replied Mr. Lennox, "but the trolleys would have to pass through a detector before moving from Canterbury's to the coffee shop which would immediately sound an alarm. Thus, the trolleys couldn't be taken out on to the street by that route without being detected. What Canterbury's customers normally did, if they wanted a cup of coffee before taking their shopping to the checkout, was to leave their trolley on the Canterbury's side of the detector, enter the coffee shop where they could buy their drink and then return to take their trolley to the checkout after they'd completed their refreshment."

At the end of the meeting, Mr. Lennox returned to Canterbury's and the detectives met to consider their strategy for solving this problem.

"I have a theory," declared Christine. "The adjoining coffee shop is the common factor which links the stores where a major spate of shoplifting is occurring. I think that what is happening is that the shoplifters are working in pairs. They go into Canterbury's with identical shopping lists and they separately buy the same items. One shoplifter then goes through the checkout in the normal way while the other takes their trolley to just outside the coffee shop and goes inside for a cup of coffee. He or she waits for their accomplice to load their shopping into their car and return to the coffee shop to pass on their credit card and the till receipt which will itemise the identical items in the trolley parked just outside the coffee shop. This receipt will be the shoplifter's passport to leave the shop without taking their trolley through the checkout as they can produce this as proof that they've paid for their purchases, should they be challenged by a member of the security staff. If the security staff investigate further, the bogus shopper will produce the credit card used to pay for the goods and the receipt will show the four digits which match the last four on the credit card. This is evidently what Mr. Lennox described to us without his realising that the till receipt produced when the customer was challenged was for someone else's identical shopping!"

"Well done," DI Whittaker complemented Christine. "Your idea makes a lot of sense. We'll pay a visit to Canterbury's to observe what happens in the coffee shop and see if anything happens to support your theory."

Nine o'clock, the following day found DI Whittaker and DS Powers drinking coffee in Café Caligula which butted on to Canterbury's. They'd been there for about an hour and were on their third cup of coffee when they noticed a fairly hefty woman with thick horn-rimmed glasses and a blue tee-shirt which seemed to claim that she had attended Ohio State University, leave a laden trolley outside the

coffee shop purchase a coffee and take a seat.
A few minutes later, another woman stepped in
to the coffee shop from the street. She was
short, stocky and wore a sleeveless navy vest
over black track-suit bottoms. Her arms were
wreathed with tattoos of hideous looking
snakes. She scanned the shop and spotted the
woman whose trolley was on the Canterbury's
side of the direct access to the shop from the
supermarket. She walked over to this woman,
passed her something which the detectives
were sure was her credit card and till receipt,
and left the shop by the street entrance without
buying herself a coffee.

Our detectives followed. at a discrete distance,
the woman who finished her coffee, collected
her trolley and left Canterbury's main entrance
without passing through the checkout. They
would not have been noticed as they recorded
the vehicle's registration number.

FM 63 NHT

They devised the mnemonic which enabled
rapid recall of the number if needed,

FIX ME   SIX THREE   NICE HOT TEA.

"There's no point in arresting her now," observed DI Whitaker. "She'll be back and my guess is that this is quite a big scam, extending over at least three shops. By careful surveillance, we should be able to identify and apprehend most if not all of those involved. We will need photographic evidence to build up a watertight case. For this, we need to discover from Mr. Lennox what security tapes can be made available."

A further meeting was arranged with Mr. Lennox and the other managers of the Canterbury's branches which were experiencing serious shoplifting. It was with great relief that these managers realised that the shoplifting scam had almost certainly been uncovered and pledged their co-operation.

"One solution to the problem," suggested DI Whitaker "would be to assign numbers to all your shopping trolleys which could be discretely entered on the till receipt by the check-out staff. This would identify a shopping load with a definite trolley and it would be something to be borne in mind should a spate of this sort of crime continue. However, I don't suggest this as a solution to the current problem. It would be extremely expensive and the fewer who know about our surveillance methods at present the better. If all the checkout staff know about this, a leak to the shoplifters is likely to occur and we will lose them. No, photographic evidence is all we will need to secure a conviction. Our surveillance may take up to two or three weeks but this will be necessary to make sure we can apprehend all the criminals involved in this heist. We will need to have from you managers, CCTV tapes which show everybody leaving the checkout section with a trolley. These will enable us to prove that on the dates concerned, the woman, or more likely, women, leaving from the café with their trolley did not pass through the checkout. We will of course need photographs of the women concerned in the coffee shop, leaving Canterbury's and loading their cars. Police photographers, skilled at taking photographs while they themselves are unobserved doing this, will provide this evidence. They have special equipment to enable them to take photographs surreptitiously. The car number we took when carrying out our initial surveillance has enabled us to find the address of one of our suspects."

The evidence was collected in the way suggested by DI Whitaker. In the event, a total of twelve women, living in the same street in a run-down part of Oakenhampton were arrested and convicted. In the searches made in conjunction with this investigation, it was discovered that the women had advertised a cut price grocery delivery service to those who were not on the internet and couldn't therefore order their grocery on-line.

DS Whitaker pointed out that the people making use of this service were technically in breach of the law by receiving stolen property. However, it wouldn't be a sensible course of action to prosecute these vulnerable elderly pensioners who could quite justifiably plead that they were totally unaware that their groceries were stolen goods being supplied by a criminal gang.

The detectives concerned were commended by the Chief Constable for the way they had brought this case to a successful conclusion.

The supermarket managers would have liked to pay a monetary reward to the police officers for solving their problem but it would have been unethical for the police officers to have received this money for doing the job they were paid to do anyway. In the end, a generous donation was made to the police benevolent fund. DS Christine Powers received a special commendation as she was the one who first deduced the way in which these thefts were being orchestrated.

Chapter 10

Joan's Curacy

So it was that Joan went to Barnholme to serve her curacy. She found Theo to be very pleasant, even charming. First impressions can often be deceptive. Joan and Annette took to each other immediately and quickly became firm friends.

Joan met Theo every morning in the church for the service of Morning Prayer. The practice of saying the daily offices in Anglican churches is a legacy of the monasticism which dominated the church in the middle ages. Some may regard the practice as outmoded but many find that it does ensure that the clergy start and end the day in prayer and read the whole Bible over the course of a year or two as they follow the passages set aside in the lectionary for daily readings. Joan was disappointed that these daily services did not include a greater element of open or extempore prayer when problems and challenges could be remembered before God but Theo didn't seem to have much time for extempore prayer. However, he had no objection to Joan starting up a weekly parish prayer meeting. This started with just the nucleus of Joan, Annette, the gentleman church warden and his wife and the lady church warden. However, as a result of Joan's encouragement, this group grew, especially among those who responded very positively to the teaching they received from Joan on the occasions on which she preached.

Apart from seeing Theo at the daily offices, Joan saw very little of her Vicar at other times. In a way, this suited Joan as she felt she had greater freedom to use her own initiatives in innovating parish activities and the Vicar was more than happy to give Joan her head while he concentrated on social activities.

The usual uniformed organisations for young people were already well established but there was no Youth Club running. Joan was able to recruit the help of two professional couples whose children did not attend scouts or guides but who were in the age bracket for which youth club provision was needed. They turned out to be ideal youth club leaders. Joan didn't neglect the uniformed organisations but often paid them a visit. She was frequently invited to close their meetings with a short epilogue.

Joan was intrigued to see the way the Parochial Church Council (PCC) ran. This was made up for the most part of elderly ladies with the churchwardens present, ex-officio. Theo's suggestions were seldom challenged and he had a very smooth run as the PCC invariably just rubber stamped anything the Vicar suggested. A minor controversy arose when the treasurer suggested that those who gave regularly and generously to the church should be encouraged to make their donations by standing order or direct debit rather than into the collection bags on Sundays. Theo opposed this on the grounds that money so donated via the bank would not be among the notes and coins consecrated as the alms dish is brought up at the end of a service. He said that he felt that this act of consecration was important.

The area where Joan made a particular impact was in her teaching ministry. Her sermons were always well prepared, challenging and very interesting. She was disappointed with Theo's preaching and surprised that the congregation were prepared to sit through his lengthy, boring, turgid monologues which were devoid of illustrations, challenge or sound teaching. The congregation certainly appreciated the contrast between Theo's sermons and Joan's dynamic style. Through her conversations with parishioners, it became apparent to Joan that most of those in the church believed that as God was a God of love, almost everyone would go to heaven and that if they did their best to live good Christian lives, they would be bound to get there. The Vicar's sermons had done little to challenge this attitude and the concept of salvation by grace alone and not by works was alien to most of them. However, in time, through the ministry of Joan, the light dawned on individual members of the congregation who discovered a personal faith in Jesus, not just as their example but as their Saviour. Joan encouraged these converts to share their testimonies and this had the effect of many more in the congregation coming to a living, dynamic faith.

Joan was concerned that those wishing for their children to be baptised, whether they were regular church members or not, just had to submit their names to the church secretary and turn up with their babies and baptismal party at three o'clock on the third Sunday of the month. Joan was able to persuade Theo that it would be a good idea if she held pre-baptism meetings with parents wishing to bring their children for baptism. However, she wasn't able to persuade him to carry out baptisms in the context of the Sunday morning services.

During the second year of her curacy, Joan made an alarming discovery. The observant nature she had developed when in the police force was a permanent aspect of Joan's make up. She noticed that after Theo received the alms dish and consecrated the collection, he slid it on to the shelf near the top of the trolley used to bring in utensils used for Holy Communion. This all seemed perfectly normal except that she noticed that after he had slid the alms dish onto this shelf, he fiddled something at the back of the trolley which sounded like a catch being fastened. She decided that she would investigate the trolley when the Vicar was on his day off. Needless to say, Joan discovered the trolley's secret.

Joan released the bolts, slid down the panel and discovered concealed on the upper shelf was an alms dish with eight full collection bags. She counted the collection, replaced it in the bags restored the alms dish to the top shelf and re-secured the sliding panel behind which this alms dish had been hidden. She then examined the church inventory and discovered that there was only one alms dish listed and eight collection bags had been written off as lost. She recorded the collections which had been taken over the past three years on to her lap top. Joan then carried out a statistical analysis of these figures. She was a good mathematician and able to deduce a lot from her analysis. The wild fluctuations from week to week of the collections could be taken into account with three years' worth of data, and her analysis indicated that statistically, the collections when Theo was away from the church were approximately 10% higher than an average Sunday. It wasn't difficult for Joann to deduce what Theo was doing. Her suspicions were confirmed when the collection recorded by the churchwardens on the following Sunday was exactly the same as the sum Joan had counted from the concealed tray. In other words, the collection counted each Sunday was not the collection taken during the service but the money on the alms dish concealed behind a panel when the trolley was wheeled into church.

The following day, Joan challenged Theo about her discovery. He blustered, saying that he had other good causes the church didn't know about to which he wished the money to be donated, a typical Theo lie. When he discovered he wasn't being believed, he insulted Joan by suggesting that they could share the money he creamed off from the collection each week. Joan was having none of it.

Joan had considered carefully what action she should take after she had informed Theo that his scam had been exposed. The obvious course of action would have been to report this to higher authority but she thought of the repercussions. Such a scandal would have done the church's reputation no good at all. A particular concern of Joan was the effect it would have on her great friend, Annette. She therefore told Theo that she couldn't work under him any more so she suggested that, preferably, he should resign his orders or, if he really couldn't do that, he should move to another parish and amend his ways. She told him that she certainly would report him if she discovered in the future that he had involved himself in any more dishonest practices.

Theo had no alternative but to accede to Joan's demand, move fairly quickly and find a parish a long way from St. Thomas's. No wealthy parish was available but Theo managed to secure the living of another very poor parish in another diocese a long way away from Barnholme. He told Annette that the Bishop wanted him to take over a challenging parish which needed some life breathed into it. It was arranged that Joan should continue her curacy under the supervision of the Vicar of the neighbouring parish church. She managed to cover the activities which were currently being looked after by Annette. The social activities which had been promoted by Theo were able to continue under the leadership of lay people.

Chapter 11

Colonel Barrington Brown

St. Mary the Virgin was the main parish church of Grimstoke. Grimstoke was a decaying town in the industrial North where once the clutter and clicking of shuttles in the busy cotton mills had been a feature of the town in its days of prosperity. Colonel Barrington Brown, a distinguished former officer in a cavalry regiment, was one of the churchwardens. He was a widower. He had retired from the army at the age of forty-five and he and his wife had enjoyed a few happy years, living in a comfortable house on the edge of the Malvern Hills. Sadly, his wife had died when only in her early fifties. Colonel Brown took stock of his life. He had enjoyed life near Malvern. He and his wife, Constance, had a circle of good friends and were prominent members of the local church. However, he himself was only in his early fifties, fit and active. He felt he had a lot to give and didn't see a future of playing golf and socialising with his affluent friends as a productive way of spending his remaining years of energetic life. Colonel Brown had a social conscience.

One morning, Colonel Brown picked up his morning paper and his eyes lighted on a survey which set out to identify the most socially deprived towns in Britain. High on the list was Grimstoke. It was categorised as an urban priority area and as such, attracted limited government funds to support its infrastructure. Its schools regularly failed their OFSTED inspections and no super heads could be recruited to rescue the failing schools. Unemployment was well above the national average and the crime statistics were not encouraging but not high. There was very little worth stealing in Grimstoke. The survey linked the plight of these deprived areas with the fact that hardly any professional people actually lived in them. Professional people so often had the get up and go which enabled town life to flourish, setting up gardening clubs, amateur dramatic and operatic societies, book reading circles, and of course, sports clubs. In particular, the churches in Grimstoke were in serious decline because, as in the similar case of schools, no-one was prepared to minister there or take a responsible part in the running of church activities.

The thought had immediately flashed through Colonel Brown's mind,
"This is where I should be."

Within a month he had sold his own house, bade farewell to his very good friends in Malvern and moved up to Grimstoke where he had had no difficulty in buying a more than adequate house on the edge of town. He joined the church of St. Mary the Virgin which was going through another of the long inter regna which punctuated the brief stay of incumbents at the church. He was warmly welcomed and was elected churchwarden within a timescale which was less than that normally permitted by church regulations. A problem he inherited was booking neighbouring clergy to come and take Sunday services.

Colonel Brown applied to become a Reader and although an older person, he still came within the age limit at which a person may be accepted for training as a Reader. Knowing the problem which existed at St. Mary the Virgin, and having nothing but glowing references from previous colleagues, his church in Malvern and the army, the Bishop had no hesitation in allowing Colonel Brown to take services and preach at church, even before he was licensed.

Colonel Brown was encouraged to find that the situation at the church was not as bad as he had expected. His associate church warden, Mrs. Violet Smith, was charming and easy to work with. She was a retired pharmacist but had remained in Grimstoke after retirement for much the same reason that Colonel Brown had come to live there. The secretary of the P.C.C. was a Dr. Henry Grey, the only medical practitioner working and living in Grimstoke. The congregation consisted very much of elderly ladies whose working lives had been spent in the once busy cotton mills but the congregation was not devoid of men who brought their families to church. The men worked in Grimstoke as postmen, shopkeepers and council employees. Quite a few parishioners commuted to the nearby big cities to work. No-one attending the church was wealthy but a very gratifying feature of the church was the generous level with which church members supported the church financially. Colonel Brown, in his privileged position of churchwarden, discovered that a large proportion of the church membership actually tithed their income. St. Mary the Virgin was always able to pay its parish share. This could not be said of some of the churches in more wealthy parts of the diocese.

It was with some delight that Colonel Brown and his fellow church council members heard that an experienced minister had actually responded to the standing advertisement for a minister to take over as incumbent at the church.

Chapter 12

Theo and Joan in their new Churches

A small contingent from Barnholme made the long journey to be present at the induction of Theo as Vicar of the church of St. Mary, the Virgin in Grimstoke. Joan didn't attend the induction. Theo and Annette were helped to settle in by Colonel Barrington Brown.

Colonel Brown conducted Theo and Annette round the grimy streets and soulless shopping centre where a third of the shops were boarded up. Miserable looking men slouched in and out of one or other of the three bookmakers located in the main street. A focal point in town was the pub, 'The Blacksmith's Anvil'. It didn't look as if renovation had been carried out on it since 'the Blacksmith's Anvil' once thrived in its Victorian heyday. The picture on the inn sign was barely recognisable as a blacksmith smiting a red hot piece of metal on his anvil and really did need to be repainted. The name, 'the Blacksmith's Anvil', was etched on its frosted glass windows. Swinging doors on loose hinges opened into a gloomy interior where both the grey marble bar top and the dirty cream coloured floor tiles were extensively cracked.

"Holy Communion services are held at eight o'clock on Sunday mornings and Morning Prayer is at eleven," explained Barrington. "We're lucky if we get more than a dozen at Holy Communion but the attendance at Morning Prayer usually tops fifty. Evening Prayer attendance just dwindled to no more than four or five and disappeared altogether during the inter regnum. I think you will find it an uphill task if you are minded to revive this service."

Theo was not so minded.

"Although our congregations are not particularly large, those who attend are very dedicated. Most of them tithe their limited incomes and on a Sunday, the total collection from the two services usually exceeds a couple of hundred pounds," said Barrington by way of encouragement.

"Poor pickings here," thought Theo to himself.

"I think there's great scope for social work here," were Annette's inner thoughts.

Theo's one and perhaps only strength lay in promoting social activities. As he had done at his previous parish, he started Bingo afternoons for the elderly. However, other things he'd successfully pioneered at his former parishes, ballroom dancing, quiz evenings and rambles didn't take off. He was however able to successfully launch a second Bingo session, this time in the evening and not primarily directed at the elderly.

The church treasurer, Mrs. Rose Underwood, ran a rudimentary Sunday School attended by twenty children who turned up regularly and seven or eight others who came on a sporadic basis. The Sunday School ran in parallel with the morning service. Annette's offer to help with the Sunday School was warmly appreciated and the new ideas she injected saw a significant increase in numbers attending. As the Sunday School grew, some young women in the congregation were recruited to the Sunday School teaching team.

Annette, Rose, Barrington and Violet Smith, the other churchwarden, met regularly for prayer. There was a lot to pray about and answers were forthcoming. Annette made a point of visiting the elderly members of the congregation, mainly ladies but a few men, who faithfully struggled to church each Sunday. From these visits, Annette had leads which enabled her to make contact with other elderly parishioners who would have come to church but for infirmity due to age or a medical condition. This led to her becoming acquainted with some of their younger relatives who were most grateful that someone from the church whom they regarded as having an official position (Vicar's wife) should go to this trouble to take an interest in their parent or aged aunt and some of these younger relatives, attracted by Annette's gentle personality, started to attend church.

As the Annette and the three main parish officers discussed the problems facing the parish, it became clear that endemic debt was a major problem among the general population of the area. They took advice and discovered that setting up a credit union was a fairly successful way of mitigating this problem. The credit union they formed didn't magically cancel people's debts but it enabled Annette and the church officers to provide advice and incentives which enabled people to regulate their finances in a more responsible way and gradually pay off the crippling loans which blighted the lives of so many in Grimstoke. So many needed to be educated in what most might consider to be fairly obvious pitfalls of borrowing. They were taking out the so called 'payday loans' without appreciating the crippling rates of interest they would be paying. So many were unaware of what was meant by APR and the explanation of the significance of APRs in excess of 50% enlightened many in debt who just hadn't considered the implication of the exorbitant high rates of interest they were committed to paying. The credit union enabled the church to provide significant help to many outside the church's fellowship who were oblivious of the fact that the church had the will and potential to help them in a very important way.

Theo hadn't learnt his lesson. As at Barnholme, he had a duplicate of the church alms dish made in secret by the firm whose services he had employed previously and he had a trolley made to the identical design of that which he had had constructed for use at St. Thomas's, Barnholme. Thus, he was able to misappropriate 10% of the collections at the Communion Services but compared to Barnholme, these were meagre pickings.

"At least," thought Theo, *"I'm unlikely to be allocated a nosey curate at this church to poke around things which were none of her business."*

The Reverend Joan Powers fared rather differently in the church to which she moved on completing her curacy. As St. Thomas's was still in an inter regnum after the departure of Theo Green, the PCC made a very strong plea that Joan should stay on as Vicar. However, the Bishop rejected this request as something which was contrary to normal church procedures. Joan had earned a considerable reputation in the diocese during her curacy and she didn't have to apply for a post. She had several requests imploring her to become their Vicar. Joan was spoilt for choice. In the end,

Joan didn't opt for the most prestigious church on offer but went to one which shared her churchmanship and where she saw there was considerable scope for development. There were a lot of good things already going on at St. Andrew's, Hollyside, but Joan was aware of other things which were needed, to develop the church's spirituality. A priority was the establishment of a weekly prayer meeting. Joan realised that it would be a mistake to rush round and start up Bible classes, home study groups, women's groups, a youth club and an alpha course and attempt to continue running all these things herself, single handed. She needed to identify those with leadership qualities to whom she could delegate the running of these activities and over the first few months in her new parish, Joan was able to assemble a formidable team of gifted leaders to whom she could safely entrust the running of these activities.

Joan also identified a number of spiritually minded people whom she considered would be an asset to the church as licensed lay readers. After a couple of years, Joan had a team of six Readers, all eager to preach and lead services.

This created a problem Joan hadn't initially thought through. Having got these people trained, how was she going to capitalise on their newly acquired skills and use them in ministry? There weren't enough services on a Sunday to keep them all busy. Joan was a lateral thinker, able to think outside the box. A vicar with a narrow vision would only consider doing those things which directly benefitted his or her own church. Joan's vision was wider. Her first loyalty lay with serving Jesus Christ over and above the Anglican Church, but there need be no clash with these loyalties. Joan had established excellent relationships with the neighbouring non-conformist churches, Baptist, Methodist and United Reformed. Of these, the United Reformed Church was struggling, having had no full time minister for the past two years. In consultation with her Readers and the elders of the United Reformed Church, Joan arranged that her Readers would carry out some of their preaching activity at the United Reformed Church. This arrangement proved mutually beneficial to both churches and the Readers welcomed the preaching opportunities which became available.

Joan inherited a gifted music group who took a leading part in the church worship and she realised that she would be able to harness this talent to organise a 'Makeway March', of the type which had been pioneered by Graham Kendrick, as a means of open air witness round the parish. This again was an initiative which she was able to share with her neighbouring non-conformist churches.

Many thought of Joan as the human equivalent of the burning bush which Moses saw in the wilderness, a person with fire in her heart, expending a huge amount of energy but showing no sign of flagging or being consumed by the fire of the Holy Spirit which burned within her.

Joan's ability to think clearly and express her viewpoint with some eloquence resulted in her being elected, first to Deanery Synod, and then to Diocesan Synod. She really was a lady who showed great potential for becoming a church leader at national level. After serving just four years as Vicar of St. Andrew's, Hollyside, Joan was appointed Archdeacon in the Diocese of Norcester. Theo's parish of Grimstoke lay within this Diocese. As archdeacon, her style of address was the Venerable Joan Powers. This seemed a strange appellation for a woman in her mid-thirties!

Chapter 13

A Diabolical Plan

The *'Reverend'* Theophilus Green was clearly concerned that Joan had become a senior church officer in the Diocese of Norcester where he now held office.

"At some stage, Joan will visit St. Mary the Virgin as part of her duty as Archdeacon. Unless I can cover my tracks, she'll discover that I'm doing much the same here at St. Mary the Virgin as I did at St. Thomas's, Barnholme" thought Theo. *"If the worse comes to the worst, I will have to take steps to 'eliminate' her before I get reported to the Bishop and then unfrocked."*

'Eliminate' was Theo's euphemism for murder!

Theo considered what options were open to him. When visiting a museum in Italy, he had once been shown a chalice, used by the Borgia popes to 'eliminate' people they considered undesirable. The handle of the chalice was designed so that it contained poison which could be released into the cup by operating a catch concealed in the handle. After drinking from the chalice himself, providing the illusion that the content of the cup was safe, the pope would release the poison into the cup and hand it to the guest he wished to 'eliminate'. Theo realised that there was a faint similarity between this original 'poison chalice' and the scam he had designed into the trolley used to convey church materials to and from the church and vestry, Theo considered getting such a chalice made for himself but the problems with using this as a means of committing a murder and remaining undetected were too great. He hit upon a more straightforward scheme.

The first problem was to identify a suitable poison and obtain a sufficient quantity to carry out his plan, should he ever need to put this into action. Theo researched the problem and found that digitalis would be the most suitable toxin. The cause of death by this poison could be mistaken as a heart attack. He found that it could be made from fairly common plants like foxglove, oleander and lily-of-the-valley but just how would he make it and test its effectiveness? Feed it to the cat? There was no guarantee that he would be able to measure the correct dose or even whether a cat would react in the same way as a human to ingesting this poison. Although he had no qualms about killing his cat, even Theo hesitated to cause Annette the distress that would result from the demise of a beloved pet.

Theo discovered that digitalis was in a rarely used medicine called digoxin which was prescribed in strictly controlled doses to some patients, suffering from heart disease. He immediately thought of old Mrs Smithers. She was a heart patient. Whenever he had visited her, her medicines were spread out on a table beside her chair along with a box of tissues impregnated with balsam and a flask and tumbler of water. There was more than a strong possibility that digoxin was included in her medication. Theo called on Mrs. Smithers who was delighted to receive a visit from the Vicar. Hers was a typical old lady's room. Some lighting was provided by a low wattage lamps in an elaborate chandelier but behind her chair was a more powerful standard lamp to illuminate whatever book she was reading. From the volume which was opened up but placed face down on her table to keep the page, it appeared that she was currently ploughing her way through 'Vanity Fair'. The bookshelves were filled with assorted leather bound novels by Dickens and Anthony Trollop along with the complete works of Shakespeare and anthologies of verse by Victorian poets. A Persian carpet square was laid across the floor centre while the edges of the room were covered by plain lino. A china cabinet displayed some pieces of cut glass and small china objects bearing the crests of once fashionable seaside resorts.

After a short interlude of small talk, Mrs Smithers asked the Vicar if he would like a cup of coffee or tea. While she was out, Theo rifled through the medicines on her table. He was in luck. There was a box labelled digoxin containing half a dozen cards of blister packed tablets. Theo estimated that a single card full of tablets should be enough to prepare a fatal dose and he took one from the box, leaving five full cards of tablets. *'One missing card won't be noticed,'* he thought as he placed the stolen card in in his pocket. After drinking his coffee, Theo left and returned home to prepare the digitalis in a form which he could administer to Joan, should this course of action prove necessary.

A week or so later, Theo received notice that the triennial visitation of St. Mary the Virgin would be carried out by Joan herself rather than the Area Dean and she requested that she might preach at the communion service on the following Sunday.

The day of the visitation arrived. Colonel Brown, the Churchwarden, had neatly laid out the church plate and valuables, the inventory and the various registers, documents and log books which churches are legally required to store safely. Joan arrived with a theological student on experience placement. She greeted Theo coldly but showed much more warmth as she shook Colonel Brown's hand. The documents were all in order and nothing included on the inventory was missing. Having completed this inspection, Joan informed Theo that she had other business to conduct with the church warden and asked Theo if he would be kind enough to take the ordinand round the church, explaining to him any things about the running of the church he might need to know,

Once Theo and the ordinand were out of earshot, Joan raised a few questions with the Churchwarden about the way services were run. Among these questions was a query about how the communion vessels were transported in and out of the church. Colonel Brown explained that a trolley was used and complied with Joan's request to describe the trolley in detail.

"There's no sign of the trolley here," observed Joan, "nor is it included on the inventory."

"That's because that trolley is the Vicar's personal property." explained Colonel Brown. " It's not here now because the Vicar decided yesterday that it was a bit scruffy and he didn't want you to see an item used in church services in that state."

"I bet he didn't" thought Joan to herself.

"Was there anything much wrong with the trolley?" she asked.

"Not really," replied Colonel Brown. "I think the Vicar was being unduly fussy."

Joan recorded the collections taken at Holy Communion services over the last few years and made a note from the service register of the Sundays the Vicar was away. When she analysed the figures later, it was clear that on average, collections were 10% higher on the Sundays the Vicar was away.

The Vicar returned to the vestry with the theological student. Joan then bade her farewell as she left with the ordinand, stating that she looked forward to being at St. Mary the Virgin on Sunday.

Joan decided to raise the irregularity she knew was being practised with Theo after the service on Sunday.

Colonel Brown disclosed to Theo what had been discussed with the Archdeacon while he was in the church with the ordinand.

"The Archdeacon will definitely have to be eliminated," thought Theo to himself.

The Sunday arrived and the Archdeacon followed the Vicar as they processed down the church at the commencement of the service. The Vicar presided. Joan preached one of her usual powerful sermons. At the end of the service when the communion vessels had been placed on the altar, the Vicar organised the ablutions. He drunk half the unused wine remaining in the chalice and handed it to the Archdeacon to empty. He then rinsed the chalice but instead of using water from the flask on the altar, he took out another similar flask from a shelf behind the altar.

(Those who have acted as servers at services of Holy Communion will know that in many churches, the altar can look splendid from the front with its covering displaying the correct liturgical colour as a backcloth to the ornate embroidery, but the back of the altar can look very different and untidy. At St. Mary the Virgin, the view of the interior of the altar from the back displayed a jumble of woodwork with a shelf along the back, just below the top of the altar. Church cleaning materials and brushes could be seen, stored at the base of space within this altar.)

Theo three-quarters filled the chalice with the liquid in this flask, held the chalice to his lips in the apparent pose of drinking and then handed it to the Archdeacon to drain the apparently remaining water from the chalice. In reality, in spite of his appearing to drink, none of this liquid, which was the digitalis solution he had prepared earlier, passed Theo's lips. On completing the ablutions, Theo replaced the flask which had contained the digitalis well back on the shelf below the top of the altar. The flask of clean water provided for the ablutions remained unused on top of the altar.

The service was over. The Vicar and Archdeacon proceeded down the aisle to say farewell to the guests as they left the service. When the last member of the congregation had left the church, the Archdeacon had intended to challenge Theo on the irregularities she knew were going on, but she was now feeling distinctly unwell. As soon as the church was empty she bade Theo a hasty farewell, promising to return tomorrow. Joan drove home with difficulty. On reaching home, she rushed to the toilet and was heartily sick. Joan flushed the toilet and went to lie down on her bed.

The following morning, Joan did not show up at the chapter meeting. This was most uncharacteristic of her. Her phone wasn't being answered so someone was sent round to investigate. The front door hadn't been locked. The milk was still on the doorstep. Joan was found lying on her bed, dead!

Chapter 14

A Very Thorough Investigation

At Oakenhampton Police station, the gap left by Joan's departure was filled by her sister, Christine, who had graduated with flying colours from Hendon Police Academy the year Joan started her training at St. Matthew's and St. Mark's Theological College. Christine not only strongly resembled her elder sister in appearance but was like Joan in so many other ways, personable, popular, industrious and very smart in appearance. It was just like having Joan back with them.

Christine was the first to hear the news that her sister had died and was distraught when she reported for duty. Most of the police officers at Oakenhampton had been there when Joan served among their ranks and there was general dismay all round that such a well-loved member of their force had died at such a young age. At that stage, Christine could not give any clear details of the cause of death.

Back at Grimstoke, the coroner ordered a post mortem to be carried out. The pathologist could not come up with an absolutely definite cause of death. The fact that Joan had vomited and flushed away the vomit before dying created a problem for him but he did say that digitalis poisoning seemed a likely cause of death. The coroner recorded an open verdict but the distinct possibility that Joan had been poisoned was sufficient grounds for the police to treat the death of one of their former colleagues as a possible murder and a very thorough investigation was put underway.

Christine asked her Superintendent if she could be seconded for a time to Grimstoke to help with the enquiry. She was told that normally, this would be very much contrary to police procedure and there was always a danger that a police officer being involved in an enquiry into the murder of a close relative could get unduly emotionally involved. However, the Superintendent said he might be able to pull a few strings, especially as Christine said that she would know some facts about her sister of which the police might be unaware, which could well be relevant to the enquiry. The

Superintendent must have been either very persuasive or had special influence in high places. Christine Powers was seconded for a limited period to Grimstoke.

She was warmly welcomed to Grimstoke by Detective Inspector Peter Sinclair and his Detective Sergeant, Graham Farmer, glad of an extra officer to help shoulder the burden of this case as they were already fully stretched, dealing with other cases on their books. If Joan had been poisoned, the timing of her death indicated that it was almost certain that she had ingested the poison at church. At their first planning meeting, DI Peter Sinclair pointed out the things which needed to be established, - suspects, motive, opportunity and means of administering the poison. If Joan had been poisoned at the service of Holy Communion, the list of suspects was narrow.

Revd. Theo Green, Vicar and celebrant,
Colonel Brown, Churchwarden,
Mrs. Violet Smith, Churchwarden,
Mrs. Rose Underwood, Sacristan,
Dr. Henry Grey who had been server at this particular service.

DS Graham Farmer wryly remarked that as all the suspects had names with an associated colour, the investigation might resemble a game of Cluedo. He was put in his place by his Inspector who knew that Christine would not want a joke to be made about the investigation into her sister's murder.

"This is not a game, Graham, so not so much levity. This case is as serious as any we've encountered over the past couple of years."

Christine came up with a sound suggestion.

"Perhaps I could go through Joan's paper work and her laptop. There may be nothing there but something of relevance may show up."

"Good suggestion, Christine, you follow that up and Graham, see if you can throw light on the source of the poison. Digitalis was suggested. It's a long shot, but one of our suspects may have been seen gathering plants from which digitalis can be derived, you know, foxgloves, that sort of thing. The last digitalis poisoning case we dealt with was old Jim Collier who wasn't really competent to administer his own medication and took an overdose of digoxin. It's a prescription only medicine so make enquiries round the local doctors and chemists to see if any digoxin has gone missing. I will have a look at our suspects' bank accounts. Money often features among the motives for serious crime."

A few days later the crime squad reassembled to review progress and all three had made what were significant discoveries.

"I couldn't find anything significant in Joan's paper work," started Christine, "but I found something very interesting in the log she kept on her laptop. It would seem that four years ago, Joan had a major fall out with her Vicar over what she described as grossly dishonest practices. She indicated that Joan refrained from reporting this to avoid the incalculable harm the disclosure would have done to the church's reputation and to avoid the terrible upset it would have caused her great friend, the Vicar's wife. I looked into church records and discovered that four years ago, Joan was serving a curacy at St. Thomas's, Barnholme, at the time under the Reverend Theo Green. He moved up here to Grimstoke before Joan had completed her curacy."

Christine continued to report something else she had discovered which may have been significant.

"There is something else on Joan's lap top which I think is of interest. There are two files in a folder labelled 'Church Collections.' These contain sets of figures which represent collections taken at both St. Thomas's Barnholme and St. Mary the Virgin, Grimstoke. Joan had carried out an analysis which indicated that at both churches, on certain Sundays, the average collection was 10% higher than the average collection taken on the rest of the Sundays. I don't know at this point in what way Sundays with higher collections might be significant."

"Well done, well done, Christine," gushed DI Sinclair. "I think we have identified a prime suspect.
Graham, have you had any luck with your line of enquiry?"

DS Graham Farmer was very excited as he spoke.

"Yes, indeed. The results of my enquiry are complementary to Christine's. I called at all the local chemists and doctors to find out whether they had missed any digoxin. The answer was negative except that Dr. Leonard Johnson reported that one of his patients had requested a repeat prescription for digoxin before her existing tablets should have run out. However, as she only had a very few tablets left and was insistent that she couldn't possibly have lost a card of tablets, Dr. Johnson repeated the prescription. He was reluctant to let me know the name of the patient concerned on the grounds of confidentiality and medical ethics. However, such considerations can be overridden in something as serious as a murder enquiry. Dr. Johnson knew Archdeacon Joan Powers well and was as keen as anyone to bring her murderer to justice if murder was indeed the cause of her death. The patient concerned was a Mrs. Smithers. When I called on her she was quite tickled to have a police sergeant coming to her for information. She has so few visitors that she had no difficulty in recalling everyone who had visited her recently. Her Vicar, Mr. Green, had called on her a few weeks ago. She thought it very unlikely that her Vicar would tamper with any of her medication.”

“I don’t think we are dealing with a normal vicar,” commented DI Peter Sinclair. “I have had a look at our suspects’ bank accounts. Nothing terribly unusual in any of them except that when Mr. Green was in Barnholme, apart from a few Direct Debits and Standing Orders, hardly any money at all was taken from his bank account. How did he finance normal household expenditure? Here at Grimstoke, his bank account looks just like one would expect it to with cash withdrawals and a number of cheques being written for purchases and household bills.”

Christine jumped in with a comment whose significance was immediately recognised.

“The files in which the collections at Barnholme and Grimstoke are recorded show that the collections at Barnholme are very, very much higher than here at Grimstoke.”

The crime squad paused to assess the implication of all the information they had just shared. The Detective Inspector summarised their findings and put forward a theory which fitted the facts.

When Joan was a curate at Barnholme, she discovered that her Vicar, Theo, was misappropriating collection money. I would suggest that somehow he creamed off 10% of the Sunday collections for himself. I wouldn't mind betting that we'll find the Sundays in the group of Sundays where the average collection was 10% higher were Sundays when Theo Green was not at church. Joan had discovered this and threatened to report her Vicar unless he changed his ways. When she came to inspect the church of St. Mary the Virgin, here at Grimstoke, Mr. Green realised that she would discover that he was still stealing money from the collection and he decided to murder Joan before his crime was exposed. He poisoned her with digoxin, stolen from Mrs. Smithers. The reason that no withdrawals were made from Mr. Green's bank at Barnholme was because he had taken sufficient money out of the collection to meet his day to day expenses. The money he stole at Grimstoke was insufficient to meet these expenses and so he had to use his current account in the normal way."

"Bingo," said the Detective Sergeant. "Shall we go out and arrest Mr. Green now?"

"No!" said the Inspector, "We haven't quite got a watertight case We need to find out how Mr. Green administered the poison and how he managed to misappropriate 10% of the collection money every Sunday. We need to ask some questions of those who were present at Joan's final communion."

Detective Inspector Peter Sinclair and Detective Sergeant Graham Farmer called first on Dr. Henry Grey. As server at that fateful service, he would have been in a position to observe the details of what went on as the sacrament was administered.

The Inspector asked him if he saw anything unusual during that service.

Dr. Grey slowly shook his head as he thought back, and then it was as if a light had dawned.

"Yes," he said, "Now I think back on that service, there were two strange things. When I cleared the altar, the flask containing the water for the ablutions was still completely full although I had seen the Vicar pour water into the chalice and both the Vicar and the Archdeacon drank some of this water before the Vicar dried the chalice with a purificator."

"Was there any other flask containing water?"

"There certainly wasn't another flask on the top of the altar when I cleared away."

"Then, where did the water used in the ablutions come from? Could a flask be hidden away?"

"Yes, it could. There's a shelf under the altar at the back. A flask could have been slipped in there. It's not a place that I would look for a communion vessel when clearing away."

"Thank you very much, Dr. Grey. You have been most helpful. Is there anything else you can recollect about the service which was in any way unusual?"

"Yes, of course," exclaimed Dr. Grey, suddenly remembering a change in the normal procedure. "We normally wheel the vessels used in a communion service in and out of the church on a trolley but on that Sunday, the trolley was not available. We carried the vessels in and out individually. I don't know why the trolley was unavailable on that particular Sunday."

"Thank you again, Dr. Grey, you have given us another piece of very useful information."

The detectives' next port of call was to Colonel Brown, the Churchwarden. Their questioning chiefly focused on the trolley. Why wasn't it in use on the fateful Sunday?

Colonel Brown explained that the Vicar had taken it home before the Archdeacon's visitation because he didn't want a scruffy piece of equipment in the church during the Archdeacon's inspection. It's interesting that you should ask me a question about the trolley because the Archdeacon was also interested in the trolley. I explained that it doesn't actually belong to the church. It belongs to the Vicar but he has loaned it to the church to make the transportation of communion vessels easier."

"Was the trolley in a scruffy state?"

"Not at all. I don't know what the Vicar was worried about."

"May we have a look at the trolley?"

"Certainly, it's back at the church now."

They made their way to St. Mary the Virgin Church and entered the vestry. The detectives carefully examined the trolley. Colonel Brown was absolutely amazed when they discovered the concealed bolts, slid down the panel to expose an alms dish bearing collection bags containing money on the previously concealed upper shelf. The detectives told the Colonel to say nothing at all to anybody about this discovery, especially the Vicar. They told him it held the key to the reason the Archdeacon was murdered and had to be kept strictly secret until their investigation had been completed.

The detectives restored the panel to the position it was in when they first looked at the trolley and went into the church. While in the church, they had a look at the altar and discovered an empty flask on the shelf at the back, under the top of the altar. They took this away for further examination.

 "Can we arrest him now?" Graham asked of his Inspector.

"No, I think we can take this one stage further and get a confession!"

Chapter 15

The Confession.

The crime squad met again and brought Christine up to date.

The Detective Inspector started the meeting.

"I have an idea which I think will extract a confession from Theo Green if you are prepared to go along with it, Christine."

"Of course I am," said Christine before she had even heard the idea, so eager was she to bring her sister's murderer to justice.

"I have heard from your Superintendent at Oakenhampton that you have an uncanny resemblance in every way, especially in appearance, to your sister. Mr. Green has never met you. I am suggesting that you dress in your sister's Archdeacon's garments and sit in the vestry of St. Mary the Virgin at a time just before Mr. Green is likely to come there himself. I gather he invariably goes into the vestry at about nine o'clock after the morning offices. It is more than likely that Mr. Green will mistake you for your sister, come back from the dead. I know that you will use your wits in directing the conversation which follows. We will be nearby, recording all that is said.

Graham immediately applauded this idea. It was a ruse which particularly appealed to him in its simplicity and its potential to completely wrap up the case.

So it was that Christine found herself sitting by the offending trolley in the vestry at quarter to nine on Thursday morning, dressed like an archdeacon. The concealed alms dish had been removed from the hidden shelf and placed on top of the trolley. She had her back to the door. After about ten minutes, Theo Green bustled in. He stopped short as he saw this figure before him and drew in his breath.

'Surely it couldn't be, he had attended her funeral, but it looked just like Joan Powers. No it can't be. Who was this person? And they've put the alms dish I hid on top of the trolley'

Christine Powers turned round and looked at Theo.

"Hallo, Theo. You look surprised to see me."

"Yes, I am, Joan, but you've changed a bit since I last saw you."

"Would you expect me to look exactly the same, considering where I've been?"

"No, I suppose not, but surely you're a ghost?"

Christine banged the top of the trolley.

"That sounds pretty solid, doesn't it?"

Theo didn't know what to say. At that point, he was unaware that his part in the murder had been uncovered. As far as he knew, Joan would have been unaware of how she had come to die. He was soon to be disillusioned.

"Why did you do it?" asked Christine.

"Do what?"

"Steal the digoxin from Mrs. Smithers and give it to me to drink?"

Theo now realised that this ghost, (surely that is what he was seeing now) knew everything about her murder.

"I knew that you would report me for stealing money from the church and I didn't want the name of the church to be brought into disrepute or for Annette to be caused any upset."

"You know that I didn't report you before for just these reasons. Why did you think I would report you this time?"

"Because you said you would report me if you ever found me stealing money from the church again."

At that moment, Inspector Sinclair entered the room, accompanied by two uniformed police officers.

"Theophilus Green, I'm arresting you on a charge of murdering the Venerable Joan Powers by administering poison. You are not obliged to say anything, but anything you do say may be taken down and used in evidence at your trial."

Theo was completely flabbergasted. His mind was in turmoil. He couldn't think straight.

"But you can't accuse me of murdering Joan. Here she is, alive and well."

"Let me introduce you to WPC Christine Powers, Joan's sister.

Theo was speechless. Christine couldn't control the anger she had repressed for so long on knowing that her sister had been murdered.

"You complete and utter bastard. How do you dare to wear a clerical collar and masquerade as a priest? You haven't just killed anyone. My sister was a truly wonderful, special woman. Few women rise to her eminence in the church and she would have gone further had you not cut her life short to avoid your dirty little secret from being exposed. May you rot in the hottest place in hell," she screamed.

Theo was cuffed and led away. Theo was tried. found guilty, given a life sentence and committed to a high security prison. He was unpopular among the other inmates and was frequently subject to assaults. Although they had never been really close as husband and wife, Annette regularly visited Theo in prison. She was concerned that he frequently bore marks of injuries he had received as a result of scuffles with other prisoners but Theo characteristically lied about how these had been sustained, claiming he performed heroic acts to protect guards from deranged prisoners. Annette knew Theo well enough to take these claims with a pinch of salt.

Particular sympathy was felt for Joan's sister, Christine, but in time she got over the loss of a sister who had been very dear to her. Christine shared so many of her sister's characteristics including her ability. She rose through the police ranks to ultimately become Assistant Chief Constable of a Metropolitan County.

Joan Power's funeral was a very moving affair. It was conducted by the Bishop in Norchester Cathedral. Although a large building, the

Cathedral could not accommodate the many mourners who flocked to pay their respects. Overflow arrangements had to be made in the Cathedral meeting rooms where the service could be relayed using closed circuit TV cameras. The many tributes paid to Joan were powerful and moving and she was granted special honours posthumously.

Chapter 16

The Venerable Charles Cavendish

A specially able young churchman was identified to replace Joan Powers as Archdeacon of Norchester. Charles Cavendish had an impressive pedigree. He could claim a distant relationship with the Dukes of Devonshire. He had obtained a first class honours degree in natural sciences at Cambridge University, a university which boasted a famous laboratory named after another illustrious Cavendish. Charles shone in his theological studies when he trained for the priesthood and after serving a curacy in a London parish, he survived a baptism by fire as incumbent of a notoriously difficult inner city parish in Liverpool. He was very much a priest in the mould of David Shepherd, a former Bishop of Liverpool, and formed excellent relationships with neighbouring churches, both catholic and protestant. His parish had suffered from years of urban decay but his pastoral work with all the communities represented in his parish resulted in considerable numerical growth in a church which had only a small congregation when he arrived. His ministry attracted members from all ethnic groups in his parish.

On his appointment as Archdeacon of Norchester, Charles Cavendish was aware that particular difficulties might be faced by the parish of Grimstoke in view of its previous vicar having to leave under a very dark cloud. How would the parishioners react to knowing that their Vicar had been found guilty of murder? Would there be a strong reaction against the Vicar's wife? Charles spent some time in the parish to identify any special support it might need. To his surprise, the Archdeacon discovered nothing but sympathy for the Vicar's wife.

"We've always felt sorry for Mrs. Green. She was far too good a person to be married to a sly schemer like Mr. Green. He was always looking out for his own interests. He was often openly rude to Mrs. Green at meetings. He just didn't appreciate the wonderful work she was doing around the parish."

This was typical of many comments made to Charles extolling the merits of Annette while disparaging Theo.

The Parish of Grimstoke was not a particularly attractive living and a long inter regnum was to be anticipated. Until the appointment of a new vicar, Annette was able to remain in the vicarage. Charles was impressed with the leadership shown by this wife of a disgraced former vicar. The church was actually growing faster than it ever had when Theo Green was vicar. Apart from his no longer appearing at services, the only really noticeable difference that Theo's imprisonment had made to the parish was the demise of the Bingo sessions. These were largely patronized by non-church members anyway. Theo preached only rarely as he could leave the sermon slot to be covered by the team of excellent Readers which Annette had been very instrumental in recruiting. Sometimes, churches within an urban priority area find it difficult to recruit good leadership among the laity but St. Mary the Virgin had two excellent church wardens and a team of really gifted lay Readers whose sermons resonated with the congregation. As Annette and her team of Readers had given considerable support to other neighbouring churches, these churches in turn were more than willing to provide ordained clergy to preside at services of Holy Communion at St. Mary the Virgin during the inter regnum. Colonel Brown was also licensed to preside at Holy Communion by extension.

During his visits to Grimstoke, Charles found himself spending a considerable amount of time with Annette and became strongly attracted to this young woman. One day, he asked Annette why she didn't divorce Theo. He had given her more than adequate grounds. However, although Annette admitted that the thought of becoming a clergy wife had weighed more heavily with her than her love of Theo in deciding to marry him, she insisted that she had married Theo for better or worse. Although his lying and failure to communicate had caused Annette much unhappiness and posed a barrier between them, Annette would not dishonour the wedding vows she had made before Almighty God.

Then an event occurred which caused a dramatic change in Annette's marital status. A senior police officer called and broke the news that Theo had been killed in a brawl with other prisoners.

Over the months that Charles and Annette had spent time together as Charles supported her in upholding the parish during the inter regnum, they had come to love each other very much. In truth, it is likely that it was a case of love at first sight at their initial meeting. Charles allowed a short but respectable time to elapse after Theo had been laid to rest before he proposed to Annette. Their marriage service was conducted by the Bishop and took place in Norchester Cathedral. It was the greatest social event of the year in the Diocese, attended not only by family members, members of the parish and neighbouring churches, but also by church dignitaries in elevated positions in the Church of England and by senior police officers who were aware that a fairly strong attachment had been established between their former colleague, Joan Powers, and Annette..

Soon after the birth of their second child, Charles was consecrated a bishop, moving

fairly quickly from suffragan status to become
a full diocesan bishop.